Haunting at Home Plate
David Patneaude

✱ 7.00

		DATE DUE	

Bridgeview PTA
2004

HAUNTING AT HOME PLATE

– DAVID PATNEAUDE –

ALBERT·WHITMAN & COMPANY

MORTON GROVE, ILLINOIS

— Also by David Patneaude —

Dark Starry Morning * Framed in Fire
Last Man's Reward * Someone Was Watching

Library of Congress Cataloging-in-Publication Data

Patneaude, David.

Haunting at home plate / by David Patneaude.

p. cm.

Summary: After they hear stories about their baseball field being haunted
by the ghost of a boy who died there many years ago, twelve-year-old Nelson
and his teammates start finding mysterious messages written in the dirt.

[1. Baseball—Fiction. 2. Ghosts—Fiction.] I. Title.

PZ7.P2734Hau 2000

[Fic]—dc21

99-40607

CIP

Published exclusively for Scholastic Book Fairs.

ISBN 0-8075-3184-7

Design by Scott Piehl.

To my mom and dad, who showed me
that reading is more than a pastime;
it's a doorway to life and dreams.
To Judy, who helped bring my dreams to life.
And to life's gifts to me: Matt, Jaime, and Jeff.

To all the grownups who take a positive
interest in kids' sports and activities.
And to all the kids who benefit.

Many thanks to Kathy Tucker, a pinch hitter
who knows how to step to the plate
and deliver when it counts.

—D. P.

— Contents —

— Prologue —
June 14, 1946

From his perch on the limb of the big cedar, Andy Kirk looks out at the diamond and beyond. Dusty black cars rumble and groan through the gate, slowed by clusters of walkers and kids on bikes. People are dressed for the afternoon sun in smiles and short sleeves and bright summer dresses. They carry blankets and picnic baskets and folding chairs and short wooden stepladders. But Andy doesn't need a stepladder. Up here, twenty feet in the air, fifty feet from home plate, no one can get in his way.

His mom and dad sit a few feet from where Andy's big brother Sam will play first base for Rivermist. He's taking throws from the infielders, fielding grounders, joking with the second baseman and pitcher. It's good to hear his laughter; for a long time Sam stopped laughing. His sense of humor was a victim of World War II, missing in action along with the blood he'd left on that far-off beach in the Pacific.

Quiet settles over the park as something big and silvery rumbles along the curve of the entrance road and emerges from the shadowy alley of trunks and branches. The bus. It squeezes into a parking space. Andy leans forward.

The word BOMBERS is painted in big black letters on the side of the bus. Above the name, a cartoon figure of a baseball player, muscles bulging, holds a bat shaped like a bomb.

The players file off the bus. They're all in full uniform—gray pinstripes and black caps. Andy wonders which one is Buzz-Bomb Borden. He's heard Buzz-Bomb is big, but all these guys look big.

Another player steps from the doorway, and right away Andy knows who he is. He's tall—maybe half-a-head taller than everyone else—and broad shouldered. His cap is pulled low, and his big jaw works side-to-side as he chews and spits. Then Buzz-Bomb Borden leads the rest of the Bombers across the grass to the diamond.

The teams size each other up, the Bombers warm up, the crowd comes alive, the mayor throws out the first ball, and the game begins.

Buzz-Bomb is famous for throwing his pitches from just in front of second base. Although Andy figures the extra distance should give the hometown guys an advantage, through three innings they get only two hits and no runs. But the Bombers haven't scored either. Kenny Johnson is pitching for Rivermist, and in 1942, when Kenny Johnson graduated from high school, people were talking about him making it to the majors someday. Instead he made it to Italy and came home with a metal plate in his head. But he still throws bullets.

The Bombers get two runs in the fourth on a couple of hits and an error, which gives Andy a chance to use his score-keeping system. He pulls two pennies from his left pants pocket and sets them in a small hollow where his big branch joins the trunk of the tree. The visitors have two runs. When Rivermist gets a run in the bottom of the fourth, he gets a nickel from his right pocket and puts it in the hollow. The home team has one. They add another in the bottom of the fifth, and Andy puts down a second nickel. It's 2-2.

Kenny Johnson shuts down the Bombers in the top of the sixth, and Buzz-Bomb strikes out the first two Rivermist batters in the bottom of the inning.

Sam steps to the plate. Andy leans forward into a little breeze, reaching in his pocket, fingering a nickel, feeling his pulse quicken. Sam hasn't gotten on base yet, but he's hit the ball hard. He's due.

On a 2 and 1 count, Buzz-Bomb throws a fast one, but Sam's ready. He swings and connects and the ball rockets away, rising over the shortstop's head, soaring toward the gap in left-center. The left fielder turns, the center fielder turns. They take off fast, but the ball's going faster. It drops on the fringe of the outfield and kicks into the cedars on the other side of the park. Sam rounds second and heads for third. Andy pinches the nickel tighter. The left fielder collects the ball and fires it toward the cutoff man at short, but Sam's heading home. The shortstop pivots and throws; Sam's sliding. He slips under the tag and across home plate and the ump spreads his hands. "Safe!"

Andy yells Sam's name, he shoots his left hand high, fingers spread in the V-for-Victory sign, he wrenches the nickel from his pocket.

He loses his balance.

Teetering back, he grabs for the trunk but can't find a hold. He sucks in a chestful of warm, sweet air and wedges his feet against a lower limb, catching himself. He overcorrects forward. His heart rises up to his throat as he stares down at grass and dirt and roots and swipes at the big branch. His fingers brush soft bark and then nothing. *Strike three*, a voice whispers to him, and suddenly he's in the air, dropping head first, squeezing the nickel hard. He closes his eyes. His last wish is for wings.

— 1 —
New Season

I walk back and forth along the riverbank, eyes on the boggy ground. I stoop and rise, stoop and rise, picking up rocks the size of golf balls and bigger. I drop them into a dirty canvas sack and head upstream, where the river narrows to sixty feet. Here the high opposite bank is pockmarked around a rotting stump that angles out from the sandy mud.

I dump the rocks on a pile of other rocks: about enough to get my throwing arm built up a little more, to get me ready for the day Mr. Conger calls on me to step to the mound and fire that first pitch. It's possible he will. My dad says if I practice, anything is possible. And if I have to practice without him, this is the best place to be.

I stand tall and twist from side to side before picking up a rock and throwing it easily toward the stump on the opposite bank. Halfway across, it splashes into the muddy water. The ripples stretch out, move downstream, and disappear.

The next rock flies a little farther, the one after that farther still. On my tenth throw, the rock reaches the bank, pocking the mud. The next one thuds into the stump, scattering mushy red pieces of wood. I close my eyes and picture a baseball thumping into a catcher's mitt: Emmett's mitt catching, my arm pitching.

I keep throwing, increasing my speed. The stump takes a beating as I rifle the stones across the water.

Finally, the pile of rocks is gone. I stop, shrug out my muscles, stare across the river at the pattern of holes in the opposite bank, fading in the March twilight. The sun has slipped behind the layer of clouds that blankets the distant peaks of the Olympic Mountains, white-capped, gray-shouldered ghosts of Washington's northwest coastline.

I pick up a flat rock from a smaller pile, then take a step forward and throw, aiming to skip it. The rock skims low to the middle of the river before setting down, lifting off, setting down, lifting off. It skips four times and plops into the mud.

As the sky darkens I skip more rocks, until I'm down to one. I pick it up, kick high, and dip low, releasing it fast and flat. It barely kisses the surface, dancing across the water and thudding into the bank. I return to my bike and pedal away from the river.

*

Pure dark has set in by the time I get to town. Waves of cold rain roll out of the sky, matting down my hair, soaking through my sweatshirt and jeans. I take the shortcut through the grounds of the junior high. At the far end of the parking lot, I stop at the sound of a too-familiar voice.

Down on the track, under the lights, two figures lean against the wind. Mr. Conger, huddled under a striped golf umbrella, growls orders to his son, Gannon, whose dark hair is glossy-wet and glued in strands against his forehead. Neither of them sees me.

I quietly angle my bike toward a small clump of fir trees. I squeeze past wet branches until my bike and I are both out of sight.

"Three more sets," Mr. Conger says. Gannon turns toward the short, steep hill that rises to a chain link fence fifty feet away. His dad raises a stopwatch. Gannon jumps up and down in place. His sweatshirt and sweatpants are heavy with rain, and they hang and flop on him like wet laundry. He lowers himself to a crouch, ready.

"Go!" his dad says, and Gannon stumbles forward, losing his footing on the slick cinder surface before reaching the grass. He sprints ahead, arms pumping, head down. He tops the hill, touches the fence, turns and jogs back down. At the bottom he drops to the track and does five quick push-ups before heading back up the hill. He repeats the routine over and over—nine more times, I count—then stops at the bottom, hands on his knees, breathing deep.

"Stand up," his dad orders. "That set was slower. You gotta maintain. Thirty seconds and counting." His dad counts down by fives to zero. "Go!" he says.

Gannon finishes this set, then another. He walks in a ragged circle around his dad, gasping for breath. Puffs of vapor hang around his head.

"Pitiful," his dad says. He drops a tall orange cone near the inside edge of the track and slumps off into the darkness. Four stripes—forty yards—away he drops another. He comes back, stopwatch raised, and waits for Gannon to line himself up with the distant cone. "Hustle!" he yells. Gannon sets himself in a sprinter's start. "Go!" his dad shouts, and Gannon takes off, churning down the track, flying past the marker.

His dad glances at his stopwatch and grunts, and Gannon jogs back to the start. "Go!" Another sprint, another grunt. Then eight more, a break, another set, a break, another set. His dad kicks the cone as Gannon staggers past it for the last time. He throws his umbrella, and the wind tumbles it to the middle of the football field.

Gannon bends over and stares at the ground. He straightens up, his chest heaving. "I did my best, Dad," he says. I can barely hear him.

His dad gives Gannon a look. "You've got one chance to redeem yourself, Gannon. Or these workouts are gonna have to get tougher. A lot tougher. We'll be spending less time at the batting cage and a ton more here." He heads back down the track to collect the far cone. "Get the umbrella," he barks.

Gannon retrieves the umbrella. His dad sets the cone at the edge of the track, takes the umbrella, and clears his stopwatch.

"A four-hundred," he says. "Under seventy."

"Seventy?"

No answer. I try to imagine running a four-hundred meter at any speed after the workout Gannon's just had. I've run the four-hundred for the school track team. I've never cracked seventy seconds on *fresh* legs. But Gannon moves to the cone. He pulls off his sweats. His T-shirt sticks to him like loose skin. Steam rises from it like wisps of smoke. He crouches, pulling up his sagging shorts.

"On your mark. Get set. Go!"

Gannon accelerates smoothly down the straight-away. Going into the first curve he lengthens his stride, fighting to stay loose. Vapor mushrooms from his mouth and trails off behind him.

He comes out of the curve and into the wind, slowing. Two hundred meters to go. He increases his speed, then backs off. He'll need something in reserve at the three-hundred mark, where the bear named Fatigue will jump on his back and ride him to the finish.

He hits the curve. A hundred to go. Time for a burst, but the bear has arrived; Gannon's just hanging on. His dad windmills his arm, urging him to speed up. Gannon raises his chin, he lifts his knees, he tries, but he's left everything behind him somewhere. He moves into the straight, forcing his legs to work. His shoes slap against the track, his arms pump back and forth in slow motion.

He staggers past the cone and stumbles, holding his stomach. He kneels on the grass. Finally, he picks up his sweats and eases to his feet, turning. His dad's hurrying down the track, umbrella angled low against the rain. Gannon shuffles after him, trying to catch up.

I'm cold, shivering, but inside I'm hot. I feel tears collecting in my eyes.

His dad sits inside the car when Gannon arrives. The motor is running. Gannon goes to the passenger side and tries the door. It's locked. The electric window slides down three inches.

"Seventy-one point two," his dad snarls. "Walk home."

The window hums back into place; the car accelerates away. Gannon watches, then pulls on his soggy sweats and heads into the darkness.

I wait, until the cold seeps into my bones and drives me from the trees and sends me home.

A big-bellied man with a tie and clipboard takes a seat on the top row of the bleachers. Chas sizes him up first.

"A scout, Nelson," he whispers to me.

A quick once-over tells me Chas is right: a scout. Either for Little League All-stars or an early bird for next year's Pony League tryouts. Who else would be spending an afternoon at North Creek Park watching kids play baseball? And he has that look: crusty but smart, able to recognize real talent. He's wearing a Mariners cap pulled low over dark shades.

Chas stands tall and fires a ball to Grady. I throw a smoker to Woody. He's short; he has to jump to snag it. Woody and Grady, whose backs are to the scout, look at me and Chas like we're nuts. Chas points to the scout, who isn't looking at us; he's checking out our manager, Mr. Conger. "Scout," Chas mouths.

Mr. Conger starts infield warmups. We outfielders

move to the outfield, where we keep one eye on the ball. The other eye is usually reserved for the team we're playing, which today is the Cardinals. But today we don't have time to scout the opponent; we're scouting the scout. We make diving catches of grounders and over-the-shoulder catches of routine fly balls. We leap for balls that are barely a foot over our heads. We make the easy look hard and the hard look miraculous.

Finally the game starts. I'm on the bench, but I'm not worried. Everyone has to play at least three of the six innings, so I'll get to show my stuff later. I hope. Mr. Conger sometimes makes his own rules. His son and nephew play more than anybody, even though the nephew, Raymond—who also happens to be the son of Mr. Maltby, our coach—is no star.

Mr. Conger's son, Gannon, is a different story altogether. And I have a feeling he'll be pitching every inning against the Cardinals. With only four games to go in the regular season, we're fighting for a top-four finish and a spot in the playoffs. The bottom-four teams stay home.

We're visitors, up first. With two outs Gannon singles in a run, but Woody pops up the next pitch for the third out. Mr. Conger lurks in the dugout with a scowl and some words: "You were supposed to wait for Gannon to get into scoring position before you took a swing, *Woodhead*."

I shrug my shoulders and smile at Woody, who looks embarrassed. If we had a choice, none of us would be putting up with Mr. Conger. Not even his own kid. I figure Woody was just trying to impress the scout, who's probably already licking his chops over Gannon. Wait till he sees him pitch. They don't call him "the Cannon" for nothing.

He gets the first two batters on strikes; the third guy pops out to left field. We don't do anything in our half of the second, and I stay on the bench while the Cannon mows down the Cardinals in the bottom of the inning.

We go down 1-2-3 again in the top of the third. Mr. Conger makes one of his brilliant observations: "You clowns are hitting like girls."

The bottom of the third starts with two easy outs, but the third guy looks like a batter—big and strong and comfortable in the box. Gannon's first pitch is down the middle and smoking, but the guy crushes the ball. It sails over the left field fence and into the woods.

The guy circles the bases, a big smile on his face,

but Gannon doesn't watch. He stares at his shoes, at the bleachers, at the gray clouds hanging over North Creek Park. He looks everywhere but at his dad, who's storming around the dugout, raking his hand through his thin brown hair. He charges the batter's box and scowls at the kid as he crosses home plate. The Cardinals' manager asks Mr. Conger what he's doing, but Mr. Conger glares out at Gannon, waiting. Finally Gannon meets the look.

"Get the next one," Mr. Conger barks. In the bleachers, the crowd is quiet. I see the scout taking notes.

Gannon's first pitch to the next guy is outside. Mr. Conger slams his fist into the chain link fence. "Down the heart!" he yells to Gannon, and my own heart thumps louder. Mr. Conger has used those words three times already this year, and three times Gannon has hit a batter who looked good. The league got wise and put Mr. Conger on probation last time. I can't believe he's at it again. Maybe he thinks he's going to fool this ump, who hasn't done any of our other games.

Gannon fires. For an instant the batter looks ready to swing. The next instant he's heading for the dirt. The ball sails into Emmett's glove, way inside and high.

The ump calls time and warns Gannon and his dad:

the next one, they're both tossed. Mr. Conger: "You heard me, ump. I called for a strike." The ump ignores him.

The batter, shaken, lets three strikes go by with the bat on his shoulder. The inning is over. Mr. Conger is smiling; Gannon isn't.

I get my first at-bat in the top of the fourth with two outs and nobody on, but I strike out swinging on a ball that's way outside. I don't impress anybody.

It's still 1-1 going into the bottom of the sixth—the last inning. Mr. Conger moves me to second base from right field.

Their big guy leads off. Mr. Conger is on his feet, glaring at him as he walks to the plate. He smiles at Mr. Conger, whose face gets redder as he takes a step out of the dugout. "Down the heart," he says to Gannon. Not loud, but the ump gives him a look. Gannon studies the ball in his mitt and waits for the batter to get set. He takes a sign from Emmett, winds, and throws. A strike, down the heart of the plate.

Mr. Conger asks the ump for time, storms to the mound, and gets in Gannon's face. Gannon nods, then stares at Mr. Conger's wide back as he turns and walks to the dugout. Gannon pounds the ball into his mitt.

Emmett gives a sign, Gannon pitches. The batter coils, but he's not ready for what's coming: a screamer, high and inside. Way inside. The ball smashes into his helmet, and he goes down.

The Cardinals' manager rushes out. I look away, back to the bleachers. My mom decided she's had enough of Mr. Conger; she's boycotting these games. Mrs. Conger is sitting there calmly. Our other parents are quiet, watching the downed kid. The scout is writing furiously on his clipboard.

I hear the ump call time. "You're gone, son," he says, and Gannon leaves the mound, head down. "You're outta here, Conger," he says to our manager. "Leave the field. I'll be filing papers."

"You can't do that," Mr. Conger says. "'Down the heart,' I told him."

"Don't insult my intelligence. The game's not resuming till you're gone."

"Hold on a moment, gentlemen." The scout is out of the stands and walking toward home plate. "Is the boy okay?" he says to the Cardinals' manager.

"He's okay."

"Take your base then, son," the ump says.

The scout stops in front of our dugout as the

Cardinal heads to first. All the guys in the field edge closer, like swimmers on the lip of a whirlpool.

"Before you go anywhere, Mr. Conger, I need to talk to you," the scout says in a loud voice.

"About what, Mr. Boggs?" Mr. Conger's voice is loud, too, but there's a little quaver to it.

"Everybody—coaches, players, parents. Get 'em in here, please."

Mr. Conger and the scout engage in an electric stare-down that seems to last forever. The scout wins. Mr. Conger shrugs and turns away. "Whatever," he says.

While Mr. Conger and Mr. Maltby call the players in, our parents file out of the bleachers and onto the field. The scout goes to the other stands and talks to the Cardinals. He comes back with the ump at his side. Mr. Conger, shifting his weight from one foot to another, looks uncomfortable. I can hear baseball sounds coming from another field behind us, but ours is dead silent.

"I'm Les Boggs," the scout says. "I sit on the board of the Southshore Little League. The board has given me the authority to represent the League in the matter before us today."

The matter before us? I glance around at a wall of blank faces.

"As most of you know," Les Boggs continues, "the conduct of your manager has been brought to the board's attention. The board asked me to attend today's game to get a first-hand impression, and if necessary, take the appropriate steps."

I watch Mr. Conger's face turn the color of tomato juice. I wait for an explosion, but it doesn't come.

"Effective immediately," says Les Boggs, "I'm suspending Mr. Conger for the remainder of the season."

"I go, my kid goes," Mr. Conger says, and I feel like someone's punched me in the stomach. I can't see Gannon. I look behind me; he's sitting with his mom, his cap pulled low over his eyes.

"That's your decision. And your son's."

"It's mine."

"Me and my kid will be going, too," Mr. Maltby says. And with that the whole good news-bad news thing hits me: we're getting rid of Mr. Conger, but Gannon, our best player, our friend, is leaving, too; without Raymond we're down to one sub; without Mr. Maltby, we don't have a coach.

"Your choice, Mr. Maltby," Les Boggs says. He looks

at his clipboard and counts to ten—the number of players we have left.

"You have some decisions to make," he says to the rest of us. "After today, you'll have three games remaining in the regular season. You have ten players to play those games. That's not much of a cushion, but if you want to keep the team together, you can do it. First, of course, someone will have to volunteer to manage."

I look at the parents. Most of them get that distracted look my dog Sunny gets when you call her. As if she's just heard something off in the distance somewhere.

"The other option is to dissolve the team," Les Boggs says. "We'd rather not see that happen, but if you can't come up with a manager, we'll have to. Because of the circumstances, we'd pretty much let the boys choose what team they'd like to play for. However, we couldn't put more than one or two of them on each existing team."

Still no one volunteers. But going to a different team, especially this late in the season, sounds like a bad idea. I ask Hugh and Kevin what they want to do. Stay together, they say, even without the Cannon. It's the one time I can remember them agreeing on anything. But most of us are friends. We all go to the same school—Moorwood. We don't want to split up.

"I'll tell you what," Les Boggs says. "Let's get this game started again. I'll sit in the dugout as acting manager. You all think about what you want to do, and we'll have a short get-together after the game and see if we can figure out some things."

Sid, the tallest guy on our team and our second-best pitcher, gets the first guy he faces out on strikes. But the big Cardinal, recovered from the shot to the head, steals second and third.

The next batter pops one deep to right field. Woody makes a clean catch and a decent throw to try to get the runner tagging up on third, but it's not even close. He scores. The Cardinals win. This is not our day.

Our record is now nine wins, eight losses. We sit in the bleachers after the game, eating cookies and drinking sodas and wondering about the future of the Dodgers. Can we still make the playoffs? Will we even be a team by playoff time? I'm feeling like somebody let the air out of me.

Les Boggs leans against the fence, looking up at us. "How many of you players want to see this team stay together?" he says.

I raise my hand. I look around. Everyone has a hand high in the air.

Les Boggs smiles. "Parents?"

The parents' hands go up, not quite as quickly or as high, but they go up.

"Good. Now we need a manager. Someone at least eighteen years old who can pass the Washington State Patrol background check. It would help if the person knew something about baseball, but we won't be real fussy." He waits. "Aunt, uncle, older brother or sister, friend?"

I look for a hand, listen for the voice of one kind person. Then I get an idea. My hand shoots up. "My cousin Mike," I say. "All-star pitcher in high school, now a premed student at the university."

"Sounds good," Les Boggs says. "What are the chances?"

"I'll ask," I say.

"What's your name, son?"

"Nelson Lamp."

"Your folks here?"

"Not today."

"Tell you what, Nelson. Talk to your cousin, or have your folks do it. If it's a go, ask your cousin to call me."

He gives me his card, I give him my phone number.

"Anyone else have any ideas?" Les Boggs says. No response. "Okay. Today's Saturday. I understand the team's next scheduled practice is Monday evening. The team can't practice without a manager." He glances around one last time. "Thank you, folks. You have your cousin call me, Nelson."

"Okay," I say. I get a ride home with Chas and his parents. I sit in the back of their van, wondering if Mike will do it.

Phantom Limb Park

My mom is happy at the news about Mr. Conger, even when I explain that the team might have to break up.

"I told you before that I'd rather not have you play, than play for that man."

"But baseball's my game, Mom." There are things about baseball that have gotten under my skin: the feel of a ball on the sweetest spot of the bat; a perfect throw; the way my cap lifts off my head when I race for a long fly ball; the smells of leather and grass and dirt.

And it's my dad's game; it's something we've shared as comfortably as a warm afternoon in our vegetable garden. It's something I can grow until he comes home. Which won't be long now, but maybe too late. He's overseas for his company again—Korea this time—and he's not due back until after the regular season ends. So we have to get into the playoffs. He's missed the whole season; he has to see me play at least once.

"I know you love baseball," my mom says. "But you shouldn't have to put up with a man like Brad Conger just because you love a sport. I'm glad the league finally did something."

"Will you call Mike for me?"

"I think your cousin would be thrilled to hear from you."

I work up my courage and go to the kitchen phone. "Is Mike...uh, Michelle there?" I say when her roommate answers.

She comes on the line. She sounds older, not like the girl who used to baby-sit me.

"Mike, it's Nelson," I say.

"My favorite little cousin!"

"Are you busy?"

"Always. I've got finals coming."

Not the answer I want to hear. I decide to plow ahead anyway. "Guess what happened to my baseball team today?"

She doesn't guess. I recount everything that went on. She seems interested but hurried. I get to the point, telling her our problem and my idea for solving it.

Silence on the other end. I wait, willing her to say yes.

"I'd really like to help you out," she says after an eternity, "but I've got my hands full here."

"You don't have to do much," I say. "We just need an adult to be there. We can kind of manage ourselves. We only have three regular-season games to go."

"Then playoffs?"

"We might not even make the playoffs."

I hear some papers rustling. "I'm sorry, Nelson," she says finally. "I'm sure one of the parents will do it, though, if they know the team will have to break up."

"They knew that this afternoon; nobody volunteered."

"Sorry. But call me again sometime, okay?"

"I will," I say, telling myself to be polite. What I feel like is whining, begging, yelling at her until she gives in. This is our whole season, this is me and nine other guys she could help out by saying yes. "Thanks for thinking about it, at least." I hang up, feeling like I let the whole team down.

"Too busy with school?" my mom says.

I nod, thinking about asking my mom to just come

and hang out while we practice. But she doesn't even get off work until we're nearly done. And my dad's on the other side of the world. When I really need him to be here, he's on the other side of the world.

I call Chas and give him the bad news. He hasn't come up with anything either. I'm about to call Les Boggs to tell him we don't have a manager when the phone rings.

"It's me." Mike. My heart does a little stall in my chest. "What kind of kids are on your team?"

"What do you mean?"

"Do they work hard? Do they get along with each other? Do they know baseball well enough that they can practice pretty much on their own? In other words, do you guys need a baby-sitter?"

I know the answers I'd like to give her, but she's my cousin. "We all come to practice," I say. "Everybody works pretty hard. We don't always get along, but we can try harder. We've all been playing since tee-ball. I don't think you'd have to baby-sit us."

I can hear her breathing on the other end. "Do you like these guys?"

"They're my friends, mostly."

She's thinking again. "When's your next practice?"

"Monday. Four-thirty."

"The other days?"

"Wednesday and Friday. Same time."

"Saturday games?"

"And sometimes during the week."

I hear papers moving again. "Here's the deal: I come to the first practice; if I like what I see, I do it, if I don't like what I see, I don't. Okay?"

"Okay! Great!"

"Where do you practice?"

"Tall Cedars Memorial Park. You know it?"

"Tall Cedars? There's a baseball field there now?"

"They just finished it," I tell her. "Just in time for us to use it for practices this season. A real field, with a backstop and benches and everything. Not that weed patch that used to be there."

"Why did they bring it back?" It's a question, but there's a frown in her voice.

"Back?"

"There was a real baseball field there a long time ago, before I was born. People quit using it."

"Well, I guess there are too many teams now. They needed another practice field."

"They should've put it somewhere else."

I'm confused. "Why?"

"The place still spooks me out."

Oh. I guess I can see why. The big trees, the way their branches blow, the shadows move, when the wind comes up. The way the park lies quiet and off by itself, as if there's no town surrounding it. There are days when I wouldn't want to be there alone, watching those shadows, listening to the creaking of the old trees. But I'm twelve; Mike's nineteen. "Why does it spook *you* out?"

"You don't know the story?"

"What story?"

"What do you and your friends call the Park?"

"Tall Cedars."

"You've never heard of Phantom Limb Park?"

The name sounds familiar. "I think I've heard something, but I don't remember what."

"Maybe I shouldn't have mentioned it."

She isn't getting off that quick, busy or not. "Oh, no, you *gotta* tell me. *Now.*"

"What I've *gotta* do is study, especially if I'm going to be managing a baseball team."

"C'mon. How long would it take?"

"Curious? Really curious?"

"Maybe." I'm not curious, I'm way beyond curious. I feel like I'm sneaking through a graveyard late at night, and I see a weak, flickering light shining from the other side of an old gravestone. I'd *have* to investigate.

"Maybe I'll tell you later."

"Later? Why not right now?"

"I've got to go, Nelson. Now let's have Les Boggs's phone number."

I give her the number. I call the other guys with the good news and warn them to behave when we practice Monday.

I try not to imagine too much about Phantom Limb Park. I'm a dreamer; I don't want those kinds of dreams.

— 4 —
Andy Kirk

On Monday I decide I've learned everything there is to learn in sixth grade. School drags by. Finally, three-thirty comes. I get to the park by four.

I cruise the edge of the woods, looking each thick cedar up and down, wondering what the name Phantom Limb means. Something feels different about these trees—sad, almost. For the first time I notice scars the size and shape of pie plates hidden among the shaggy strips of reddish bark.

Besides Mike's story, I've got something else eating at me: what will the team think of her? Just before four-thirty I see her little car pull into the parking lot. She gets out, grabs some bags from her trunk, and hurries toward us. The guys are staring as she gets to the infield.

"We've got this field," Grady says to her. He doesn't share, not even stuff he doesn't own, like baseball fields. Things he *does* own, like his two-hundred-dollar Easton bat, are strictly off limits.

"We're waiting for our manager," Woody says, trying to make himself look taller.

Mike grins at me. "You didn't tell them?"

"I guess not."

I see some lights come on. "She's a *girl?*" Sid says. "Our new manager's a girl named Mike?"

She drops the bags and sticks out her hand to Sid. "I'm Nelson's cousin Michelle. Mike's my nickname. You can call me either one of those or Coach. What's yours?"

Sid stares at her for a minute. Mike isn't real tall and doesn't weigh a lot, but something about the way she carries herself makes her look bigger. "Sid," he says finally, and shakes her hand.

She's introducing herself to the rest of the team, and everything's looking good, when Hugh crowds in front of Kevin to shake Mike's hand. Hugh has the bulk to crowd in; he's as tall as I am but outweighs me by twenty-five or thirty pounds. Kevin's just a little guy, but wiry. And he has an attitude, especially when it comes to Hugh.

"You're in my way, *Huge*," Kevin says. "I'm sure she wants to meet me first. And you're blocking out the sun."

"Don't call me that," Hugh says. "You can't always be first. You're not any better than me."

"Yes I am, *Huge*, and you know it. Everybody knows it."

Hugh gets this look in his eye. He scowls at Kevin, his fists clenched at his sides. Mike just stands there, looking back and forth at them. But the rest of us know what's coming. We expand our little circle to give them some room. So much for us getting off on the right foot with Mike.

Hugh charges Kevin and wraps him in a bear hug, then they struggle for a few seconds, staggering around and grunting. Kevin gets a hand loose and lands a bunch of punches, but Hugh's bulk wins out. They take a couple of clumsy steps, teeter, and crash to the dirt. Kevin squirms to get away but can't; Hugh has him pinned.

"I can't breathe!" Kevin shouts. "Get off me, Huge!"

"Make me, runt. And the name's *Hugh*."

Mike looks ready to step in, but Emmett gets there first. He's our catcher and he's built like one—not very tall, but stocky and thick-necked. He grabs Hugh by the arm and drags him off. Sid helps. I get in between the warriors to help keep them from going at it again. Mike moves in next to me and gives both of them the eye.

I can't believe it. Their stupid little feud dates back to last season, when Kevin made the Dodgers, a major league team, and Hugh didn't make majors. He spent another year on a minor league team, and Kevin rubbed it in. They've been battling ever since, off and on, even though now they're teammates. Why couldn't today have been an off day?

I'm afraid Mike thinks I lied to her; I'm afraid she's thinking, What next? She looks us over until everyone's eyes are on her and the only noise in the park is a bird song from somewhere high in the trees. "Nelson didn't mention that I'm a girl, but I'm guessing he did tell you that today is kind of a trial run," she says to us. "I'm in college, and I've got some tough classes. If I decide to manage your team, I'm going to have to spend part of each practice studying. That means I don't have time to referee fights between a couple of guys who aren't acting their age." She looks at Kevin and Hugh.

"I've played a lot of ball," she says, "and I find I have the most fun when my teammates and I are playing well together. To play well, you have to practice hard. And you guys are going to have to practice hard on your own. If getting to the playoffs is your goal, you'll have to work hard as a team to get there."

I look around. Everybody's listening.

"That's my speech," she says.

"What about the story?" I say. "Phantom Limb Park?"

The other guys look at me, like, Where did that come from?

"You guys should be practicing," she says to me. "I should be studying."

"I've been waiting three days," I say.

She grins. "Come with me, guys."

She leads us past the first base line, past the fence, to the fringe of the cedar grove. She stands next to a tree that's thicker than she is tall. I glance up at the lacy greenery hanging from its stout branches.

She puts her hand flat against the bark and studies

our faces. "Anybody already heard this?"

Guys shake their heads no. Nobody says anything.

"This stand of cedars—173 of them—has been here forever. The park, too. In 1946—right after World War II—a baseball team from Rivermist played here against some barnstormers—the Bombers—who traveled around the country taking on locals. The whole town turned out to see the game. It was tough to find a viewing spot, especially if you were short. A kid named Andy Kirk climbed one of the cedars—this cedar—to get a better look. He climbed high, close to twenty feet off the ground, they say. He sat up there on one of those big branches where he could see everything."

I look up. One of the limbs grows as thick as a man's thigh straight out of the trunk for maybe ten feet before it elbows up toward the roof of smaller branches overhead. It's the one; I know it is. I can't take my eyes off it.

Mike continues: "With the score tied 2-2 in the sixth, Andy Kirk's big brother—one of the local guys— drove the ball deep to left, all the way to the trees. He slid home safe, and the crowd went crazy. But when the noise died down, they heard a woman screaming.

Andy had fallen. The woman who witnessed it said he lost his balance and fell just after the run scored. He hit the ground head first, breaking his neck. He died on the spot."

I hear some nervous laughter. I wait for Mike to laugh. This must be some kind of tall tale. She doesn't even smile. I get an empty feeling in my chest.

"Really?" Sid says.

"June 14, 1946. My Grandpa Leo was here that day. He says they called the game right then. They took Andy's body away. Everybody went home."

"Why Phantom Limb Park?" I ask.

"I'm getting to that," she says. "After the accident, someone came here during the night and cut off every branch that was lower than fifteen feet. There were tree limbs and sawdust all over the place. Whoever it was wanted to make sure nobody climbed any of these trees again."

"They didn't find out who did it?" Sid says.

"Andy's dad, they suspected. But it was never proven. After that someone started calling the place Phantom Limb Park. It caught on, at least for a while."

I look around at the trees. None of them has branches I can reach.

"People stopped using the field," Mike says. "Nobody scheduled games here anymore. Grass and weeds overgrew the diamond, the backstop and bleachers fell apart. Finally, they hauled everything away, and the baseball field vanished. It became just another corner of the park, like it was never here." She looks around at the freshly landscaped diamond, the grassy outfield, the benches and fence, the tall pole lamp behind the shiny new backstop. She looks at her watch. "We've got to get to work."

I do some math in my head. "Andy Kirk died over half a century ago," I say. "It still spooks you out?"

"Things have happened," she says.

"What things?" Chas says. He pushes his glasses up on his nose as if the answer to his question is in front of him somewhere, but out of focus.

"I'll tell you another time. We've got to get practicing."

She ignores our protests and leads us back to the infield, where she dumps out the bats and balls and the rest of the stuff, and asks us our usual routine. It sounds fine, she says. Get to work.

We know what to do: stretching, warmup jog, infield practice, outfield practice. Every time a disagreement over who does what starts building to a fight, we look over at Mike. She's sitting on a bench, reading and taking notes, but we see her glance up at us. We settle the disagreement.

Sid pitches batting practice. With ten players we've got barely enough: nine in positions, one at bat. Each one of us gets up, gets some smacks on the ball, runs the bases, then takes a spot in the field.

Twice Mike gets involved: once she tells Grady to shorten up his backswing; once she tells Hugh to cut off a throw from right field.

Finally it's Sid's turn to hit, which means Chas, the only other guy who's actually pitched in a game, has to pitch to him. Sid waits patiently, then impatiently, while Chas throws ball after ball—high, low, outside, inside. No strikes. Sid swings at one that comes close after about ten pitches, and misses. He waits through five more pitches, then slams down the bat.

"Can anyone here get the ball over the plate?" he says. No one says anything. I tell myself I'm not ready. A rotten stump's not the same as a plate with a batter protecting it. I wait for someone else to volunteer.

"Just swing at whatever," Kevin says from his spot at first.

Mike steps onto the diamond, wearing her glove. "Let me give it a try." She tosses a few warmups, then waves Sid back into the batter's box. She throws a couple that are just outside, then one low, almost in the dirt, that gets by Emmett.

"Mind if I go underhand, Sid?" she says.

"Not at all." Sid grins. I know he shouldn't.

"Ready, Emmett?"

"Ready."

She takes her fast-pitch stance, winds up, windmills her arm, and delivers. The ball rockets in, smoking, and Sid watches it go by with the bat on his shoulder. It pops into Emmett's mitt, moving him backward. He comes up waving his hand like it's been burned. Sid digs in, his jaw set. All eyes are on Mike.

She gets back in her stance. "These baseballs move pretty well," she says. She winds up and throws, but this one comes in at a slower speed, and each one after it is a little slower until Sid gets his bat on one, popping it foul behind him. "Shorten up your backswing, Sid," she says to him. He fouls off another one. She walks to the batter's box and adjusts his setup. He's a righty, but even from my spot at third I can see his bat's flatter, his hands are more in front of his chest.

Mike returns to the mound. She pitches and he lines it right back to her. "Mad at me, Sid?" she says. He smiles. She throws another one, a little faster, and he grounds it past Hugh. The next one's faster, but he meets it and lines it just foul down the first-base line.

"Good," she says. "Infielders, work on your run-downs, outfielders on hitting the cutoff man. Chas, work with Emmett on getting the ball over the plate. We need more than one pitcher on this team."

She goes back to her bench, but I see her looking at us more than she's looking at the book. Finally she walks back to the infield and calls us all in.

"I like most of what I've seen here today, guys," she says. "So I've decided to go ahead and manage this team for the rest of the season."

I look around and see a lot of smiles, I hear a lot of guys saying, "Yes!"

"Thanks, Mike," I say.

Mudders

Wednesday arrives, gray and drizzly. At recess I see Gannon, who tells me that he and Raymond both ended up on the Expos, the first-place team. But Gannon doesn't look happy; he doesn't sound happy. He asks a lot of questions about how the team's doing. Great, I tell him, but I'm not sure he believes me. He knows how we'll miss him.

"I hear your cousin's your manager now," he says. I nod. "Mike."

"Is she nice?" he says.

"Kevin and Hugh got into a fight at practice," I tell him. "Mike decided to manage us anyway."

"My dad would've foamed at the mouth," Gannon says. "He would've been on them like fur on dogs."

"She didn't do anything ugly. She didn't even yell."

"You guys are lucky," Gannon says.

"How's your new manager?" I ask.

"My first practice is tonight," Gannon says. "I'm keeping my fingers crossed."

By the time I leave school I'm afraid Mike has canceled our practice. A fine, cool rain is still falling, and the sky is dark to the southwest. But I head for the park. Kevin and Hugh are already there, but at opposite sides of the diamond, avoiding each other, not even making eye contact. It looks like they haven't patched things up yet. I walk toward the trees, looking for some shelter, and find myself standing under the tree. I look up at the elbow branch, imagining Andy's view of the field, what it would be like to sit there on a summer day with a big crowd down below and nothing to do but watch baseball.

The other guys come on time, and I'm glad because Mike shows up right at four-thirty.

"Nice to see you're all here," she says. "You guys looked like mudders to me, so I didn't bother telling you that we won't cancel practice if it rains. I promise you none of us will melt."

When we get to batting practice, Webb struggles. Mike moves into the batter's box with him and repositions his bat, his arms, his shoulders, his feet and knees. He takes a couple more swings but still doesn't connect.

In the field he's a master shortstop, speeding to ground balls and line drives and eating them up like candy. We call him "the Web." But he doesn't hit well. He almost never gets his bat on the ball in a real game, and when he does, the ball never gets out of the infield. Mr. Conger called him a victim at the plate. And I think he made Webb believe it.

Mike takes the bat and tells Webb to watch from behind the backstop. She settles in, coiled and compact, her head as still as a stone. "You've got to concentrate on the ball," she says, loud enough for everyone to hear. "That means no movement, no distractions." She looks out at Sid. "Bring it, big Sid," she says.

Sid winds and throws but it's outside. She doesn't budge; he looks nervous.

"Just throw strikes," she says. Sid winds and throws, and it's not his usual batting practice pitch; this one has some heat on it. But Mike waits, then uncoils, her bat a blur of gray metal. There's a solid thud, and the ball screams over Hugh's head and into the gap in left-center. Sid throws again, and she lines it over second base. The next one rockets into the left-center gap again, but deeper, almost to the trees. Her swing—the way she attacks the ball—is the same every time, as if it's programmed into her.

She hands the bat to Webb and helps him into a stance again. "Just you and the ball, Webb," she says. Sid's first pitch has good speed, but Webb waits, steady as a statue, then swings and connects, popping it straight up and high in the air. He hits the next one solid and lines it into center. He's smiling; Mike's smiling. When he blasts the next one into the alley in right-center and takes off around the bases, he's got some bounce in his step.

When it's Sid's turn to hit, Mike lets Chas try pitching, but then she gets up and takes over. Sid's last poke comes to me on the fly in right field, and I fire it back to her on the mound.

As she's heading back to her book she says, "You've got a strong arm there, little cousin. Ever think about pitching?"

"No," I lie. I've thought about it every time I've chucked rock after rock against that far riverbank, every time I've gone into my windup in front of the mirror, standing tall and staring down a hitter.

"You should think about it," she says. I almost ask her if I can throw some batting practice. Almost. But then just the prospect of being alone on the mound, throwing at a real batter, paralyzes my mouth shut.

With about fifteen minutes to go till the end of practice, Hugh tags Kevin hard during a rundown drill. It's like someone poured gas on a fire. Kevin slaps the ball out of Hugh's hand, and it hits the dirt and rolls twenty feet away.

"Pick it up, runt," Hugh says.

"Make me, Huge," Kevin says, and most of us hear that little invitation. We hurry to where they're standing between first and second, but we get there too late. Hugh attacks, head down like a bull, and Kevin steps aside and sticks out his foot. Hugh sprawls face first on the ground, and before he can turn over, Kevin is on him, trying to land a punch and hold Hugh down at the same time. Hugh bucks and twists, but Kevin hangs on to Hugh's shirt with one hand like a rodeo cowboy and tries to do some damage with the other.

Mike gets there before the rest of us. She drags Kevin to his feet. Sid and Emmett haul Hugh up from the ground like a big sack of laundry. He glares at

Kevin; Kevin glares back. Both of them are plastered with mud.

"I don't know what the problem is with you two," Mike says, "but your teammates don't have time for this, and neither do I. Practice is over." She throws the equipment in the bags and drives off.

Everyone else leaves; I stay, feeling shortchanged on practice. And embarrassed. How are we going to win if we can't practice, if we can't get along? And if we don't win, we won't make the playoffs; my dad won't see us play. Not this season. And by next season, his company might decide he's needed in Antarctica, or on Mars.

And Mike didn't get to finish her story—the *things have happened* part, the part I want to hear.

I breathe in the moist air and an overpowering sense that I'm really not alone in this place. The sense isn't new, it's been here all along, winking at me, poking me in the ribs. I just never recognized it before.

– 6 –
The Giants

Friday's practice goes better. Mike pitches batting practice to Sid again; he makes good contact with the ball. Webb gets some solid pokes. Hugh and Kevin argue but don't fight. Mike tells us we look like ballplayers, and to get some sleep for the next day's game. But I have a hard time sleeping that night. How are we going to do without Gannon? And Mike *still* hasn't told us the rest of the Phantom Limb story. She has to study, she keeps saying. Later, she keeps saying.

Saturday morning I get out of bed early. My mom's downstairs, drinking coffee in the kitchen. She glances up from the newspaper. "Do you care if I come and watch the game today?"

"It would be great. If we beat the Giants we'll be two games ahead of 'em for the last playoff spot, with only two games to go. And I figured something out: if we get to the championship game, Dad will be here to see it."

"How are you doing these days without him?"

"I'm okay most of the time. Most of the time I'm in school, and he'd be at work even if he had a regular job."

"What about the other times?" she asks.

"It's hard to get better if you don't have someone to practice with, to tell you what you're doing right and wrong," I say. "Especially right."

"Your dad's good at telling you what you're doing right."

"Yeah," I say. "And until Mike took over the team, all we had was Mr. Conger telling us what we did *wrong*. I don't know how Gannon can take it."

"He probably thinks he doesn't have a choice."

"I guess he doesn't." I think for a minute, allowing myself to dream. "Maybe Mr. Conger and Dad could trade jobs. That would get Dad home and Mr. Conger out of the country. Everyone's problems would be solved."

"Except the people in the other countries." My mom smiles. I laugh.

I decide to change the subject. "You ever hear of Phantom Limb Park?"

Her smile fades. "Not for a while."

I start peeling an orange from a bowl of fruit on the table. "You ever hear anything spooky about the place?"

"There are some stories. Your father used to tell them to you when you were little. I told him to stop; they were scaring you."

My father doesn't tell me stories much anymore. It's hard to tell a good story by e-mail.

"Talk to Mike," my mom says. "She told your Aunt Laura she had a strange experience at the park once. She can tell you about it first-hand."

Strange experience? No wonder Mike says the park spooks her out. Even though I'm standing in my own kitchen in broad daylight, I'm suddenly getting spooked out myself. And I'm not even sure why.

*

The Giants have a pitcher named Tyson Strong.

And he is. He's big-chested and tall and fast. And just as strong at the end of a six-inning game as he is at the beginning. Mike sees us eyeing him while he's warming up. "Don't let him intimidate you," she says. "Be a hitter when you go up there, concentrate on the ball, and shorten up on your stroke. If you need to, choke up on the bat a couple of fingers. You just want to meet it and force them to get you out. Okay?"

We say okay, but I don't see a lot of confidence in the guys' faces. Mike reads the lineup, and we're pretty much in our same positions: Chas in left, Grady in center, Woody in right, Nate at third, Webb at shortstop, Hugh at second, Kevin at first, Emmett at catcher, and Sid pitching. I'm on the bench. As usual.

"I'm not picking on you, Nelson," Mike says when we get to the dugout. "I just don't want the rest of the guys to think I'm going to give you special treatment. Okay?"

"I'll get to play as much as they do?"

"Everybody plays the same."

Nothing much happens the first two innings. Tyson and Sid each give up a single. Sid gets ours—a screaming line drive up the middle. He looks more confident at the plate. And Mike's really into it. She paces, shouts encouragement, talks to everyone on the team. Positive stuff. Things we never would have heard from Mr. Conger.

Third inning. I take Woody's spot in right, excited to be out there. For once, I know nobody's going to yell at me if I make a mistake.

Grady makes the mistake. A line drive gets by him, and two runs score. Chas, drawn to left center on the line drive, stays there after Grady throws the ball back to the infield. For a second I hope Chas is telling Grady that it's okay, that everyone makes mistakes. But Chas is finger-pointing and yelling something, and Grady is hanging his head, trying to walk away. Neither one is paying any attention to what's going on in the infield. The next batter is standing at the plate. He lifts the first pitch into left, to the spot where Chas should be. The ball hits the vacant spot and rolls all the way to the fence, the batter ends up on third, the runner scores. We're down 3-0 when Sid strikes out the last guy.

As Chas stands in the on-deck circle, Mike brings Grady out, and the three of them have a discussion. I can't hear what she's saying, but I have an idea. Emmett's thinking the same thing. "Let's give each other some encouragement out there," he says.

Chas whiffs the first two pitches, both high, and someone from their bench yells at him to get thicker glasses.

"Let's go, Chas!" Grady shouts, and Mike smiles. We all start yelling encouraging things. Chas bloops one over the first baseman's head for a single. He steals second and third and scores on the overthrow. We're down 3-1 when we take the field again.

The Giants get nothing off Sid in the top of the fourth, and in the bottom of the inning Sid drives in Hugh with a double to left. Nate strikes out. Then it's my chance to do something, but I get caught looking at a third strike. I can't believe it. I go back to the dugout. Nobody but Mike says anything. "Swing at the close ones, Nelson. You've got to protect the plate with two strikes."

"It wasn't close," I say, but I know it was. I sit alone on the end of the bench.

Emmett hits one back to the mound for the third out. It's 3-2, Giants.

They get nothing in the fifth; neither do we.

Top of the sixth. The Giants get runners on second and third with one out. Tyson smashes one my way, deep. I take off, looking back over my left shoulder. I see the ball dropping. I track it down and make the catch ten feet from the fence.

I turn. The runners tag. I fire toward home, giving it everything, and the ball flies on a line. I see it kick up a puff of dirt and it's in Emmett's mitt and he's laying a tag on the runner as he slides home. The ump's thumb goes up. He's out!

I hear the cheering as I jog back in. I can't help but grin. I sit on the bench, charged. I did something right. We're still only one run down.

"Lucky throw," Chas says. His mouth has the bad habit of running off in the wrong direction. I'd like to give him something nasty right back, but I hold my tongue. Mike's giving us the eye.

Webb leads off. Against Tyson he shouldn't have a chance, but he drives the ball over the second baseman's head. He's on first, eyes sparking. He doesn't look like a victim. We give him a cheer. Mike, smiling, sends Kevin out to coach first. She *should* be smiling; Webb wouldn't be out there without her.

Hugh and Sid strike out, but Webb steals second. With first base open, the Giants decide to pitch around Nate, who's a big guy and swings a mean bat. He walks on four pitches.

My turn. The count goes to 3 and 2. "Be a batter, Nelson!" someone—Chas?—yells from the dugout. I check my grip and wait, eyes squinted against the sun. Tyson goes into his windup—a big windup. A big pitch on its way. I begin my swing, timing it to meet his heat. But halfway through, with the bat flying over the plate, I realize something awful: it's not his fastball. The bat goes through, my hands and wrists follow, my whole body corkscrews. I watch the ball float by like a small white balloon.

"Strike!" the ump says.

I see Tyson raise his hands and smile. I hear the cheers. They're like the sound of a dentist's drill. I walk back to the dugout, numb.

"Nice swing, Nelson," Chas says. I look for Mike, hoping she'll chop him down to size, but she's out on the field, ready to shake hands. I get behind her and the rest of the guys and trudge past the line of Giants, slapping fives. They're smiling and saying good game; I can barely talk past the lump in my throat.

Tyson is last. "Good game," he says to me.

"You, too," I try to say. It comes out squeaky, like a little kid's voice. "Nice pitch."

"The Cannon's not the only one in the league with

a change-up," he says. "Don't always look for the heater."

Good advice, I figure, but it's hard to think about my next at-bat without forgetting this one. The Giants have tied us for the fourth playoff spot, and I made the final out. I head toward the stands, where I see my mom.

"Great throw home, Nelson," she says. The throw. I've forgotten it. I'm glad she decided to come.

7

Messages

T he rest of the weekend I try to think about positive stuff: we still have a chance for the playoffs, three teams are completely out of the race, and one of them, the Mets, is our next opponent.

But baseball's not the only thing on my mind, and I don't want to wait forever to get my answers from Mike. Saturday night I e-mail my dad with some questions. Sunday night I get a response:

Hi, Nelson (and you, too, Hannah)!
It's lonesome over here! Phantom Limb Park, huh?
I guess you're old enough for the story now. Anyway, it sounds as if Mike has given you all the basics already. I have a couple of things you probably don't

know. One is a story that was handed down about Andy's coins. Whenever he went to watch a baseball game, he always took twenty coins—ten nickels and ten pennies— to keep score. He'd use nickels for the team he was rooting for, pennies for the other team. But after he fell, they found only fourteen coins—seven pennies and seven nickels. In 1972 a kid discovered another old penny half-buried in a hollowed-out space under a root. The other five weren't found, though, and some folks believed Andy had taken them with him to that big baseball field in the sky. But lots of people started looking again.

"When I was about your age, I was in the park by myself one evening in June, on my hands and knees, searching for the coins. It was a thing kids did back then when there wasn't much else to do. It started raining, light at first but then heavier— big, warm drips coming down on me. At first I was thankful I was under the tree; I figured I'd *really* be getting wet if I were out in the open. But then I looked out. The grass was dry; through the treetops across the park I could see the sun setting. I looked up at the branches of the cedar, and they were wet, dripping. I thought of tears, and Andy Kirk, and I ran. I didn't look back. I didn't come back alone for a long time…"

My mom looks at the e-mail and shakes her head. "He hasn't lost his knack for storytelling," she says.

I have to agree. But something in her eyes, something about the hollow feeling in my chest, makes me believe it's not just a story.

Monday arrives rainy and cold, but by mid-afternoon the sun breaks through. I ride my bike the half-mile to practice.

The air hangs cool and still in the park. It's quiet. The houses and stores just outside the park entrance seem far away. I think of coins, of warm rain in the shadow of trees.

When I get to the field, Hugh and Kevin are already there. They're not fighting; they're standing at home plate, studying the dirt. I lean my bike against the backstop and walk over to them. Someone has written something: foot-high letters, deep into the soft ground. I read the words:

DODGERS—WINNERS SUPPORT
THERE TEAMMATES.

SAY SOMETHING HELPFUL OR KEEP
YOUR MOUTH SHUT. –AK

"A.K.?" I say. "Who wrote this?"

"A.K.," Hugh says. "Andy Kirk's initials."

"Sure," I say. "Who got here first?"

"We came together," Hugh says.

"Did you guys look in the trees? Somebody's probably hiding in there."

"We looked," Kevin says.

We look again, sneaking through all 173 cedars that border the field.

I look for footprints. There are hundreds of them in the infield. The other guys come, one at a time. They all deny writing it. I watch their faces for clues, but I don't see anything. Chas accuses me of doing it. I laugh at him. "Hugh and Kevin were here before me."

"You could've left and come back. You rode your bike."

"Most of us rode our bikes," I say. "We all could've left and come back."

"Mike," Hugh guesses.

"Looks like something a manager would say," Emmett says.

"It doesn't look like a grownup's writing," Kevin says. He's right. The letters are all capitals and not real steady. "There" should be "their."

Sid looks around the circle of us with a grin on his face, as if waiting for the writer to confess his joke. "Whose writing, then?" he says, but nobody confesses.

We're all staring at the words as Mike drives up and hurries over. She smiles and looks around. "Who did it?"

I shrug. "Some of the guys thought it was you," I say.

She laughs. "Not me. But I think whoever did it has the right idea. I heard some things at Saturday's game that you should never hear between teammates." She looks around at our faces. "I'd like to thank the guy who wrote it—Mr. A.K."

Still no one says anything. I study every face. Not a hint.

"None of you guys did this, really?" Her voice has an edge now. She drops the equipment bags. "Let's take a little walk, guys."

We follow her over to the tree. I think about what it would be like to hit the ground head-first from twenty feet. An instant of pain, and then nothing. Forever.

Mike leans her back against the trunk. "Last week I told you some stuff about this tree, this park," she says. "I didn't tell you everything I know." She looks at me. "When I was your age my team would come here once in a while if our regular practice field was too swampy or being used. But I didn't like it. I knew the story of Andy Kirk. I'd heard about strange things happening."

"Messages?" Hugh says. "Had there been messages?"

Mike shakes her head. "Not that I knew of." She looks up at the sky. "The last time we came here was a day like this one: blue sky, small white clouds. Then suddenly the air changed. The clouds drew together, turned gray, dropped lower. All of us stood out in the middle of the park, staring up at the sky. It grew darker, especially back in the trees.

"I was looking up when the first raindrop hit my face. A few seconds later it was pouring, then the wind came up and blew rain sideways at us. The cedars were swaying and creaking.

"We grabbed our stuff and ran for our manager's van. We piled in and he headed out. By the time we got to the street, the rain had stopped. Our manager pulled over to the curb in front of Wilson's Drug. Across the street, the flag at the post office was drooping straight down. The wind had died, the white clouds and sun had returned. The street was pretzel dry.

"A big gray cloud bank hung over the top of the park, tangled in the treetops like cotton candy. As we watched, it lifted and moved off slowly to the east, toward the mountains. Our manager took a look at us and decided we wouldn't go back. We didn't. Ever."

We study Mike's face, searching for a hint of a smile. But she's dead serious.

"That night I told my dad what had happened," she says. "He didn't act surprised. He took me into the kitchen and pointed at the calendar. 'Today's June 14,' he said. 'Andy Kirk died on June 14.'"

Uneasy but encouraged, I tell my dad's story about the rain and the coins, the five missing ones. The guys chatter nervously and look at the grass and root around at it with their shoes. My dad's story happened in June. June 14? I figure today's date: May 23. Three weeks to go.

"So you're saying some kind of ghost—Andy Kirk's ghost—really wrote that message?" Chas asks Mike.

"I don't know who wrote it," Mike says. "I do know Andy Kirk was a baseball fan. He was a baseball player. I think he'd know what it would take to play as a team."

Quiet, we go back to the field. When Hugh gets on Kevin about missing a grounder, we tell him to shut up. Mike goes back to her books, except for pitching batting practice to Sid. She's smoking 'em in faster, and he's still making contact. The guy's getting to be a hitter.

I look up at the sky from time to time, half-expecting a bank of clouds to come rolling in.

8

A Ghost?

Tuesday after school, Sid, Emmett, Chas, and I head over to the public library to find out about Phantom Limb Park. The librarian gets us microfilm of the Everett and Rivermist newspapers from June and July of 1946.

Emmett finds the first article, front-page news in the June 15 *Everett Herald*. The *Rivermist Citizen*, a weekly, reports the story four days later. We read both papers.

We find out that Andy Kirk was thirteen years old, loved playing and watching baseball, had a paper route, and an older brother named Sam. According to the paper, Mike's story is correct: Sam was the player who scored the run just before Andy fell. Seeing it in print makes the story even creepier.

Andy's picture—the same one—is in both papers.

He looks like a regular kid—round face, a smile, light-colored hair.

The next big story is in the June 26 *Rivermist Citizen*. During the night of June 21, someone went to the park and sawed off every branch growing within fifteen feet of the ground. The reporter interviews several of the townspeople. Mutilation, one person calls it. Revenge, someone else says. If you've seen one tree, you've seen them all, another guy says, and if Andy Kirk's father did it, they should let him be.

Another article mentions the missing coins. A suggestion has been made to rename the park "Tall Cedars Memorial," in honor of Andy. The reporter compares the trees to soldiers. "Proud amputees," he writes, "standing as determined sentinels over the spirit of a young boy, phantom limbs reaching out, seeking our forgiveness."

*

I'm the last one to arrive at practice on Wednesday. I race in on my bike and see the guys standing in a clump near home plate. My heart misses a beat or two.

I push past Nate and Grady. The first message is gone. In its place are two others:

TREAT EACH OTHER LIKE YOU'LL NEVER
BE ALL TOGETHER AGAIN. YOU WONT.

DON'T GROW OLD OR DIE YOUNG THINKING
ABOUT WHAT MIGHT HAVE BEEN.
ALWAYS GIVE IT YOUR BEST. –AK

"Who was here first?" I say.

"Me and Grady," Chas says. "But we're more concerned about who got here last—you."

"I was at our neighbor's having a snack," I say. "Call her."

"We might."

"I'm the one guy with an alibi, Chas."

"'Treat each other like you'll never be all together again,'" Emmett reads, and Chas and I back off.

"Maybe it *is* a ghost," Kevin says. No one laughs.

Mike arrives. She looks at the message. "Someone's showing some smarts," she says, trying to smile, looking around at our faces. But no one takes credit. Her smile flattens into a thin line. She goes to the bench and her books as practice starts. A cloud of thoughtfulness seems to have settled over the field.

Practice goes well. Mike doesn't say it, but we all know we'll have to hit better and score a bunch next game. Because she's worried about overworking Sid's arm, Chas will be our pitcher. I wonder about telling Mike I want to give it a try. I know I can throw the ball harder and straighter than Chas. But can I pitch? I don't say anything.

On his last at-bat, Sid smashes one into the alley between center and right. I chase it down from my right-field spot, knowing he's running, and catch it on the bounce. When I turn toward the infield, he's halfway between first and second. I nail him sliding into the bag.

"Great throw, Nelson," Grady says. Mike's giving me the thumbs-up from the pitcher's mound. "A strike, Nelson!" she yells. A river throw. A stump-buster. Could I take that experience to the mound and make it work?

That night I e-mail my dad and tell him about the messages. My mom thinks someone on the team is writing them, and I think she's right, but I want to see what my dad says.

He must have been looking for some mail from us, because I don't have to wait long:

Hi, Nelson!

The plot thickens. My first thought was Mike, but she has a serious respect for the park, and she's too straightforward to beat around the bush. If she wanted to tell you guys something, she'd just do it. I'm sure she agrees with the messages, though. Sometimes it takes someone to spell out the truth for us before we see it. I wish I knew your teammates better; right now I don't. But you must know them pretty well. Look around the next time you're at practice and try to find the player who cares most about other people as individuals, who believes you need to get along as a team, and who is smart and creative enough to come up with the idea. That's your guy. Say hi to your mom for me. I miss you both a ton. Love, Dad.

No easy answers from my dad. I think most of us care about each other and the team. As far as smart, the only one of us who qualified for the TAG program at school is Grady, so he's Talented And Gifted, but I don't know how creative he is. And I'm not sure how smart you have to be to write messages in the dirt, to misspell "their." But I'll keep an eye on Grady. And everyone else. I go to sleep that night parading the suspects through my mind. My dad didn't mention the ghost of Andy Kirk, but I don't eliminate anyone.

— 9 —
A Message for Mike

Friday. I go straight to practice from school. I want to be the first one there. On my bike it's five minutes to the park. No one's there. I ride to the spot, expecting the same messages. But new ones are scribbled in the dirt:

SECOND CHANCES ARE AS RARE AS RAINBOWS.

SID IS A BATTER NOW. YOU ARE A TEAM. ASK MIKE TO PITCH BATTING PRACTICE TO EVERYONE—AK

Mike's going to *love* the second message. The other guys show up one by one and give their opinions. Some of them think I did it; some think it's the ghost.

Woody, eyeing the trees, says we should try to get a different place to practice. Chas comes up with a new theory: the culprit is a parent, sneaking over here while we're in school, when parents are on the loose.

"How would a parent know what Mike's been doing at practice?" Nate says. "Or how Sid's been hitting?"

"Maybe their kid told them about practices," Chas says.

The sun glints off Mike's car as it squeals into the parking lot. She walks over and stares at the dirt. "The writing looks the same," she says.

"'Ask Mike to pitch batting practice to everyone,'" Emmett reads, using his most reasonable voice. "What do you say, Coach?"

"I've got finals coming," Mike says. But she doesn't say no.

"It would help us," Nate says. "Look what it's done for Sid."

"'Second chances are as rare as rainbows,'" Emmett says. "Maybe this will be our only chance."

Mike stares at the words a minute, blows her hair out of her eyes. "Okay," she says. She's trying not to smile.

Everyone lets out a big cheer. Except Sid. "I don't

like it," he says. When he throws back his shoulders and sticks out his chest, he's as tall as Mike.

"Why not, Sid?" Mike says. "I'll still pitch to you."

"I won't get to throw as many pitches."

"You can get some extra work during the rest of practice," she says. "And we don't want to overwork your arm, anyway. It's a team thing, Sid. Like the note says."

Sid shrugs. "Okay."

Mike walks to the mound, pitches a few warmups to Emmett, and waves Sid to the plate. He looks good again. He doesn't miss until she starts burning them in. We all watch, checking out his setup, his swing.

Chas's first swings are big and loopy—the opposite of what Mike's been showing us—and he misses badly. She walks to the plate. She gets him to flatten the bat, positions his hands out in front of his chest. She goes back to the mound and starts over. He misses the first few, but then gets some solid hits. He's smiling when he runs out his final poke, a deep fly that Grady hauls down in center field.

She pitches to the rest of the guys, helping them with their setups when they need it. Everybody hits.

Finally, it's my turn at bat. The dark background of

cedars makes it easy to focus on Mike, and her first delivery looks relaxed, but the ball comes in fast, and I miss it. Next pitch, same thing. I get just a piece of the next one. She walks to the plate, moves the bat, adjusts my hands.

"Your feet are lined up well," she says; I'm grateful *something* was right. "Without moving anything, take a look at your setup."

I look at where everything is.

"Good," she says. "Now try to remember it. And shorten up your backswing. You just want to meet the ball. Then follow through."

Her next pitch is down the middle. I swing and feel the bat hit the ball. Not solid—a pop-up to second—but at least I hit it. I connect on four in a row before Mike's speed gets to me, and I whiff a couple. She throws me a change-up, and I'm way early, practically screwing myself into the dirt.

"You're not chopping wood," she says. "You need to be aware of the change."

She throws me a fast one and I meet it. Her next pitch is another change-up, but this time I wait on it and drive it over Webb's head into left.

"Better," Mike says. "Run on your next hit."

She comes back with a toned-down version of

her heater, straight down the middle. I take a good swing and poke it between first and second. It gets past Woody in right, and I make it all the way to third, smiling.

I glance at the stand of cedars, at the big tree. I give a little nod. If Andy Kirk is writing the messages, I want to thank him.

10

The Mets

All Saturday morning I'm nervous. I put on my uniform at nine o'clock; the game's not till noon.

My mom drives me to North Creek Park. The Mets have a couple of pitchers throwing. I watch them from the outfield; they don't look like much. We beat these guys the first time we played, but the first time we had the Cannon. Now we have "the Chas." Not exactly an even tradeoff. And if Chas goes up in smoke, who do we have for a backup? Mike says she won't use Sid unless it's an emergency, since he pitched six innings last game.

We're visitors, up first. We score five runs in our half of the inning, but Chas struggles on the mound; the Mets get four in theirs.

I get a solid single to left to lead off the second, and score the first of three runs. The Mets get four again, but Chas hangs in there. We outscore them in the third inning as Sid and Woody both hit one over the fence. Our bats have come alive. Chas thinks it's the Mets' shaky pitching, but I think facing Mike in batting prac-- tice has made the difference.

I get a double in the fourth, driving the ball almost to the right field fence on the fly. We get two runs. They get three.

The score's tied 14-14 going into the top of the sixth. A football score. It's our last chance to put some space between us.

I walk to start the inning, Sid singles, Woody walks. The bases are loaded. Emmett strikes out. Chas comes up. "Come on, guys, let's hear some chatter," Mike tells us.

We get loud, Chas digs in, squinting out at the pitcher. The ball sails high and inside. Way inside. At the last instant Chas tries to duck away but it's too late. The ball thuds into him and he goes down.

Mike runs out. Chas sits up, rubbing his shoulder. Mike moves his left arm around, then Chas does it by himself. He gets up and trots to first, grinning at the applause, adjusting his glasses. I come in from third to score. We're up by one.

Grady singles home Sid and Woody. We're ahead, 17-14. Our bench celebrates, but Nate lines into a double play to end the inning. We have to protect a three-run lead.

I'm on my way out of the dugout when Mike motions to me. She's talking to Chas. My heart stalls.

"It was my other shoulder, Mike," he says.

"I know. But you've gone five innings. You've thrown a lot of pitches. You're still okay?"

Chas looks at me. I can see he's curious about why I'm there. I'm curious about why I'm there. "I'm fine," he says.

"How are you feeling, Nelson?" Mike says.

"Great." Why shouldn't I be? Chas was the one who got knocked down. But I get this gnawing feeling in my guts anyway. Is she really thinking about putting me on the mound *now*? In *this* situation? I'd rather have the *stump* throw rocks at *me*. If this is an emergency, shouldn't she be talking to Sid?

Mike studies me for a second and then turns back to Chas. "Okay, Chas," she says. "But you need to let me know if you get tired out there." She looks at me again and the gnawing feeling gets worse. "We can find you some relief."

"Can I go, Mike?" I say, but my feet are already moving. I'd like to be running.

She smiles. "Go ahead, Nelson. Get us some outs."

The feeling in my insides eases as I jog out to right field. But something else fades away, too—a kind of *what if* feeling that had me wondering and excited.

Chas walks the first guy. The next batter pops out, but then they load the bases with a single and a walk. The next guy swats one into the alley between Woody and Grady. Two runs score; runners are on second and third. I see our playoff hopes blowing away with the infield dust. Mike pulls the outfield way in, almost like a second set of infielders. I move to the hole between Nate and Hugh.

The next batter swings and it's headed straight for me, not quite a line drive, not quite a fly ball. A fungo. I get a jump on it and charge, hoping it will stay in the air long enough for me to get there. I concentrate on the ball but see the runner hanging at third, not sure if I'm going to catch it on the fly. If I do, he has to tag.

I don't, but I'm going full speed when I catch it on a short hop and whip it toward home with everything I've got. I watch it fly, low and fast and straight, as the runner goes from third. Emmett crouches, reaching for my throw. The ball pops into his mitt and he pivots toward the runner, who's just beginning his slide. No contest. He's out by six feet. Emmett scrambles up, checking out the base runners. The batter stands at second. The other runner's on third. Two outs. One to go. The cheers from my teammates and the crowd are loud in my ears. I can hear my mom yelling my name.

Mike goes out to talk to Chas. She walks back to the dugout. He pitches. The kid swings and pops it straight up. Emmett throws off his mask and staggers around home plate, eyeing the ball.

He makes the catch. He leaps and shouts, and the rest of us head for home, where we celebrate our win. We're still alive for the playoffs.

11

Nightmares and Dreams

Sunday evening Emmett and I ride our bikes to the park. We wander over to the spot by home plate. The old message—*Ask Mike to pitch batting practice to everyone*—is pretty much trampled out. There's no new message. If there's going to be one for Monday's practice, it will have to show up that night or the next day. I feel chilled as we ride home in the twilight.

I check for e-mail from my dad—an answer to my latest—but there's nothing there. I tell myself he's busy over there, he has to go places, it's a different time zone, even a different day. Still, an uneasy feeling grows in me as darkness comes.

I go to bed but wake in the blackest part of the night with the weight of a nightmare sitting on my chest. I sit up, gulping air, remembering: my dad's voice, calling my name from deep in a thick, shadowy forest of giant, shaggy trees. He's lost, and I'm tripping through tangles of roots and underbrush, trying to find him. But something moves, shifting and twisting beneath my feet. I stumble to a stop and look down through a layer of soupy ground fog. I see a mossy root tear itself from the dirt and lift into the air. Two pennies are embedded in it like shiny, coppery eyes. I stagger back, but the root snakes out to me and twines around my ankle and I fall, down and down, listening to my dad's voice fade and disappear.

Awake now, I shiver, breathe deep, and slip out of bed. I grab my dad's photo from my dresser. In the dark I can't see his face, but I hold the picture close while I roam through the house, upstairs and down, telling myself that everything's okay. He'll be flying home on a big plane, and big planes don't get lost. And me? The carpet is warm and solid beneath my bare feet; there's nowhere for me to fall.

I think of Andy Kirk, falling down and down, not in a dream, in a real-life, twenty-foot nightmare. How hard would it be for me to climb that pitcher's mound? How far could I fall?

By the time I get back to my room, my brain is convinced that I've just had a nightmare; my heart isn't quite sure. My heart beats anxiously; it murmurs for my dad, for Andy. But I get in bed and close my eyes and, eventually, drift off to sleep.

I wake up in the morning with a dull headache and a leftover feeling that something isn't quite right. But I check the computer, and suddenly I feel better. I have e-mail from my dad:

Hi, Nelson!
It sounds as if your team is coming together. I wish I could be there to see the games. And the messages. Still no clues on who's leaving them? Whoever it is has a pretty good handle on baseball. And life, too. I don't recall seeing a rainbow since I've been over here. Maybe it's not the place for rainbows. Or second chances. But you guys are still working on your first chance. I hope you make the most of it. I really want to see you play, which by my calendar means you're going to have to get into the playoffs. Not such a tall order for dynamite players with a dynamite manager. And I bet none of the other teams have a mysterious mentor on their side! Please keep writing. I love hearing from you.
Dad.

That day, Sid, Emmett, Chas, and I spend a lot of our class time talking about our victory and wondering about new messages. After school, we bike to the park. We're the first ones there. Kind of. There are two new messages carved in the dirt:

HOW MANY DODGERS DOES IT TAKE TO WIN A BALL GAME? TEN!

NELSON HAS AN ARM. GIVE HIM A SHOT AT PITCHER. —AK

The first one is okay. The teamwork thing again. The second one puts my stomach in a knot.

"Did you write this, Nelson?" Sid says. He doesn't look happy. He's scheduled to pitch the next game.

"Why do you think it was me?"

"No one else is trying to horn in on the pitching."

"*I'm* not trying to horn in on the pitching. I don't *want* to pitch."

"Sure."

Chas doesn't look pleased either, but he doesn't say anything.

"I think it's a good idea," Emmett says. "You guys

have seen Nelson's arm in the outfield. What if he could pitch like that?"

What if I could? I think about the idea as the other guys arrive, as they jaw it back and forth. Sid isn't the only one who thinks I wrote the message, but more of them are considering Andy Kirk's ghost. I can tell by the way their eyes wander off toward the trees. I can't help sneaking a look myself. But when I do, I feel as if I'm looking through an open doorway into a dark, musty room. I close the door and turn away, back to the faces around me, the conversation: most everybody agrees with Emmett—I should have a chance to pitch.

Mike shows up. The air seems to lose its chill. "Another message?" she says. She reads it and eyes me, then the big cedar. She forces a smile. "Wow!" she says. "Can you guys believe this?"

"I think Nelson wrote it," Sid says.

"I don't think so," Mike says. "Nelson hasn't been interested in pitching. But I've been thinking he should try it. He does have a slingshot for an arm."

"I think it's a good idea," Emmett repeats. "He stings my hand from the outfield."

"I don't like it," Sid says. But he's overruled. Everyone else but Chas is for giving me a try. Chas just shrugs.

"Let's do it," Mike says, and suddenly I'm nervous but not bad-nervous. Mike wants me to give it a try. Most of the guys want me to give it a try. Whoever wrote the message wants me to give it a try. And Andy Kirk? I think he'd want me to give it a try, too.

"'How many Dodgers does it take to win a ball game?'" Emmett reads.

"Ten!" everybody answers.

Mike has me warm up with Emmett while the rest of the guys have fielding practice. I start out aiming the pitches, throwing soft, just trying to get the ball over the plate, trying to ignore the tight feeling in my throat. Mike comes out and gives me some tips. "Think of it as playing catch with Emmett," she says. She goes back to her books, but I see her watching me. I'm about to start again when Sid walks over from first base.

"If you're going to pitch, you need to look like a pitcher," he says. He shows me his stance, his foot placement on the rubber, his windup, his push-off, his follow-through. I look over at Mike; she sticks her nose back in her book, but there's a smile on her face.

I throw. It's not a strike, but it's close. I throw some

more. I start feeling comfortable, like when I was at the river, alone, busting that stump. Emmett gets down in a crouch. The balls fly off my fingers and snap into his mitt, mostly right around the plate. Sweat drips from my forehead. My arm feels loose. I throw harder. Emmett puts on his protective gear. He gets back in his crouch and gives me the thumbs-up sign. I turn around and kick at the dirt and pretend to examine the ball against the green background of cedars. My teammates are all watching. The field has gone silent.

I take a deep breath and smoke one down the middle. Emmett smiles and fans his mitt as if it's hot. Somebody laughs behind me, but I barely hear it. Emmett and I are in our own little world.

When I go to right field, Sid and Chas take turns pitching to Emmett. Then it's batting practice, and Mike waves me in. "You looked good out on the mound, Nelson," she says. "Want to throw some batting practice?"

"Okay."

Afraid I might hit Nate, I'm way outside on my first pitch. This is different than going at the stump. Way different.

"Throw to the target," Mike says from behind me.

I stare in at Emmett and his big mitt. I wind and throw, and the ball sails down the middle. Nate takes his cut a little late, as if he wasn't expecting a strike, and fouls it off to the first base side. I throw another strike and he drills it to left. I throw one inside that he passes up, then one outside that he goes for and dribbles straight back to me. I throw two more over the plate, increasing my speed a little. He swings and misses the first, and drives the second one to right. I'm feeling better; I'm throwing strikes.

"Good job," Mike says to me as she steps on the mound to pitch to Webb.

I take turns with her on Webb, Hugh, Kevin, and Chas, then she sends me back to the outfield. I don't want to go, and it must show on my face.

"We don't want to burn out that arm," she says.

At the end of practice she confirms the rumor some of us have heard: the Giants, without Tyson Strong on the mound, lost Saturday's game. We're back in sole possession of the fourth playoff spot. We just have to win our next one, which is Thursday against the Cubs.

When I get home, my mom's at the computer, looking at another e-mail from my dad. This one's to her, mostly. I think about my nightmare, thankful again that he's not lost. He misses us, he says, but he'll be home soon. I'm glad. I e-mail him back and send him the latest news, the latest messages, and what it all means: we're still in the race for the playoffs, I'm getting a shot at pitcher.

He might get to see me on the mound.

12

True and False

I have to figure out who's writing the messages. And because I suspect pretty much everyone, I decide to do it on my own. Tuesday night, nine-fifteen, approaching dark, I ask my mom if I can ride to the park. I tell her I left one of my baseballs there.

"It's nearly dark," she says. "Nine-thirty. No later."

I hurry out the door before she can change her mind. In five minutes I'm there, cruising silently through the entrance, eyes bugged open in the failing light. Nobody's on the baseball diamond. I ride straight for it.

There's no new message, and the old one is pretty much history. I push my bike toward the tree. I figure I've got five minutes until I have to head out.

It's darker behind the tree. Its bark smells like the incense they burned at my Great-Uncle Joe's funeral, where the priest talked about the cedars of Lebanon. I wonder if those faraway cedars smell like this big old tree, whether they've ever seen a boy die.

I wait, hoping to see something. I hear the sound of a car cruising slowly along in the street. *I imagine it entering the park, lights out. It's a classic: big, and black, with a tall, shiny grill, and chrome bumpers. A man gets out, wearing an old, wide-brimmed hat. He opens the trunk and pulls out something long and shiny and toothy with handles on both ends: a cross-cut saw. He lays it across his shoulders and starts for the trees.*

Shivering, I get on my bike and head for home. I see no one.

*

I'm determined. The next morning I'm out of bed before sunup, waiting for the first show of light over the Cascades. When it comes, I knock on my mom's door, tell her that I'm going for a quick run.

"A run?" she says through the door. "Now?"

"I need to get my legs in shape for pitching."

"Why don't you wait till it's lighter?"

"I'll be too hungry by then. Can I go?"

She opens the door and examines me. I'm wearing my Dodgers jersey and cap, shorts, running shoes. I'm holding a flashlight.

"You look like you're ready," she says.

"I've got lots of energy," I lie.

I head out. I have to talk to my legs to get them to move. But the air breathes fresh—cool and full of some kind of tree smell.

By the time I get to the park, my eyes are used to the dark, and the sky's a shade lighter. Nobody's there. The tall lamp behind the backstop puts out enough light to show me that. But I know as soon as I take a few steps onto the infield that something has changed: a new message has been scraped into the dirt on one side of home plate:

BEWARE OF HIGH LIMBS.

And on the other side, practically under my feet, is another one:

PITCH THE ROOKIE AGAINST THE CUBS. -AK

I look around the field, wondering who would have this much confidence in me. I half-expect one of the guys to show up and decide for certain I'm the mysterious writer. Me standing there plus these messages equals one conclusion. I make tracks for home.

All day I have to act dumb. To make sure I have an alibi, I invite Emmett to go home with me after school before we go to practice.

We're almost to my house when he says, "Do you think there'll be a message today?"

"I don't know," I say, but then I wonder if that's what I should have said. Is that what I would have said if I didn't have a guilty conscience? "There's been one every practice for a while," I add.

"You think it's a ghost? Andy Kirk's ghost?"

A guilty guy or a guy with a guilty conscience would probably say yes. "I don't really believe in ghosts," I say. Not sheet-wearing, float-through-the-air ghosts, anyway. I never used to believe in any kind. Now I'm not so sure.

"I think Mike believes," Emmett says.

"Maybe."

I time our arrival so we show up not too early, not too late. When we pedal up, Hugh, Nate, and Woody are standing at the usual spot, eyeing the ground.

We ride to the spot. The messages in the dirt are clear:

BEWARE OF HIGH LIMBS.

GIVE CHAS A CHANCE AT CATCHER. —AK

I don't believe what I'm reading. I look around at the other faces and nobody else is surprised. But they didn't see the original. Why should they be surprised, unless one of them is the real message writer? I look closely. The writing on the second message looks different. Of course. Does anyone else notice? I have to fight back the urge to tell them. How could I explain it? Who would believe me?

A minute later Chas rides up, red-faced and out of breath. I stare at him, looking for some kind of sign. He looks too innocent, too dumb. He looks like a thief. He's stolen my chance to pitch.

"Another message, guys?" he says. He adjusts his glasses, as if he's trying to make out the words. "How did the message guy know I've been wanting to try catcher?" He gets off his bike and makes a big show of examining the writing. "'Beware of high limbs,'" he says. "I think it really is the ghost of Andy Kirk."

"Do you?" I know who left this phony message.

Mike's car pulls into the parking lot. I think about telling her, at least if I can get her alone. I run to help her with the equipment, but Emmett tags along.

"Thanks, guys," she says as we shoulder the bags. "Another message today?"

"See for yourself," I say.

I watch Mike's face. She's surprised to see this message.

"Catcher, huh, Chas?" she says to him.

"Yeah."

"You been wanting to play catcher?"

"I'd like to try it."

"No reason you can't, in the right situation. It depends on what's best for the team."

"Sure," Chas says.

"Did you tell anyone else you wanted to play catcher?" Mike says.

"A couple of the guys, maybe."

The other guys show up, one by one: Grady, Sid, Kevin, Webb. Mike looks around at all our faces. "Any of you guys know Chas wanted to play catcher?"

Blank looks, shrugs, heads shaking, a few no's.

Nobody says yes.

"They forgot, probably." Chas's voice sounds mat-ter-of-fact, but his eyes look worried. "Or they don't want to say."

"Does anybody see anything unusual?" Mike says. I wait, hoping someone besides me can see the differ-ences. Mike waits while we study the dirt, then the other faces in the circle. Mike's eyes are on Chas.

"They're not the same," Sid says finally. "They're pretty close, but the writing's different in the two mes-sages."

Heads nod in agreement as everyone looks again.

"The second one looks copied," Emmett says, and now all eyes are on Chas. He tries to smile, but it doesn't work. His face reddens, he looks at the ground.

"Chas?" Mike says.

"I wrote it," Chas whispers, and I feel sorry for him.

"What was the real message?" Mike says.

"'Pitch the rookie against the Cubs.'" I can barely hear him.

"'Pitch the rookie against the Cubs,'" Emmett says, loud, and the attention shifts to me.

"It's my turn to pitch," Sid says. "I'm supposed to pitch against the Cubs."

Mike ignores him. "You erased it?" she asks Chas.

"I erased it," Chas says.

"After school?"

"Uh-huh."

For a long moment nobody says anything. Finally, Emmett speaks up: "'How many Dodgers does it take to win a ball game?'"

"Ten!" we answer. We look at Chas.

"Ten," he says.

"And the team has to come first," Mike says. "Chas, you might get to play some catcher. But next time, just let us know when you want to try something different. Okay?"

Chas nods. He looks embarrassed, but I see a bit of a smile in his eyes.

"Sid," Mike says, "if Nelson keeps showing us he can be a pitcher, he's going to get his chance against the Cubs tomorrow. Maybe not the whole game. Maybe we'll need you two to split time. Whatever's best for the team. Okay?"

"Okay," Sid says.

We get started, finally. I'm taking pitching turns with Mike when an unexpected visitor shows up: Gannon. He sits on Mike's bench in his Expos cap and watches as I take over. Suddenly I'm nervous. Nate comes to the plate.

I don't want Gannon to see my best stuff. I get a nice easy one down the middle and Nate connects. I toss three more and he makes contact each time, knocking two of them deep to left.

Nodding toward Gannon, Mike says, "Is he one of the ones you lost?"

I say yes, the good one. She calls over to Gannon. "We could use another batter," she says. "You want to get in some swings?"

I'm hoping he'll say no. I'm not ready to pitch to Gannon.

"No, thanks," he says after a moment. "I'll just watch."

We go through the rest of practice. We look good, even though everyone's a little distracted by our audience.

Mike calls us over to the pitcher's mound. "He looks human to me," she says. "And you guys are good enough to play with any human."

I wonder. We give ourselves a cheer and I walk over to my bike.

"How's the Expos?" I ask Gannon.

"Okay," Gannon says. "They're a good team."

"So are we," Sid says.

"I know," Gannon says.

"Your manager," I say. "What do you think of him?"

"Smitty's a nice guy," Gannon says. "He knows baseball. Except now it's like I've got two managers. My dad hasn't exactly backed off. I'm getting advice from two directions all the time." His face darkens, as if he's stepped under a cloud.

"We are, too," I say. "Only for us, it's good. Come here a minute." Gannon follows me over to home plate, where the remains of the day's messages are still visible in the dirt. I tell him what's happened and recite the messages, real and phony. Everyone else is gone by the time I'm done.

He remembers a message and repeats it. "'Don't grow old or die young thinking about what might have been.'" He's quiet for a while. "I think some grownups think that way. They think they can relive the past through their kids. Change it, even."

"Like your dad?"

He doesn't answer for a while. Finally he says, "I don't want to be like that—full of wishes, too old to use 'em, taking it out on someone else."

"'Second chances are as rare as rainbows,'" I say, looking over at the tree. Gannon follows my gaze. "I think some adult wrote the messages."

"Maybe," I say. "Or someone who never got to be an adult."

We get on our bikes and head for the street, not talking. "You didn't look like a rookie out there pitching today," he says finally.

Pitching. It's not where my mind was, but my thoughts shift gears in a hurry. I get a nervous throb in my chest thinking about standing on the mound against the Cubs the next day. But I look at Gannon's face and see this no-nonsense expression that tells me he meant what he said. It's good to have him around again. "Thanks," I say.

That night I e-mail the latest developments to my dad. He must have been close to his computer, because he gets right back to me. He tells me how much he'd like to be there, and wishes me good luck. "I'm thinking about that 'Second chances are as rare as rainbows' message," he says, but I don't know what he means.

— 13 —
The Cubs

Game time. Make or break time for the playoffs. My mom's in the stands. I'm waiting for Mike to announce the starting pitcher. My mouth's dry, I've got this twisted-up feeling in my stomach. Half of me's hoping she'll call my name, the other half's praying she won't.

She gets us together in the dugout and starts calling out batting order and positions. "Batting third and pitching will be Sid." Sid's expression doesn't change. "Give us three good innings, Sid, and Nelson will relieve you." She looks at me. "That way we'll have both of you guys available for the playoffs. Okay?"

"Okay," we answer. Sid forces a smile. I'm having a hard time standing still.

"You're batting fourth, Nelson, and starting in right field," she says.

I nod. I hear her call Nate's name but the rest of the lineup's a blank. *I'm going to pitch.* "Fourth inning," I mouth to my mom. I make a pitching motion. She grins. We beat the Cubs last time, but it was tight, something like 5-3, and Gannon knocked in three of our runs with a homer. We don't have Gannon now, but we've got Mike. We've got our bats working. I'm feeling better about pitching, especially when Emmett tells me, "I'm going to have fun catching you."

Webb digs in at the plate. Two weeks before, he'd stand up there with the bat on his shoulder and hope for a walk. Mr. Conger would try to get him to crowd the plate, hoping he'd get hit with a pitch. Now, thanks to Mike, he looks like a hitter.

He tags one hard. The shortstop knocks it down, but has no chance for a play.

It's a good start, and we end up with three runs in the first. But in the bottom of the second the Cubs get two and have a guy on third with only one out. I creep in on the grass to have a chance to cut down the runner. The batter swings and the ball flies toward me. I start in. Too late, I realize he's crushed it. I stop, begin backpedaling, then turn and take off. I see the ball, but it's coming too fast. I leap, my glove stretched out backhand.

I crash, staring helplessly at my empty glove. Grady hustles over and fires the ball to Woody, but by the time he relays the ball to Emmett the batter is crossing home plate. He has a home run. Kind of. It should have been an out. Instead they get two runs.

"Way to hustle, Nelson!" Mike yells. The guys join in, trying to tell me I did a good job. Yeah, right.

Sid gets the next two batters. The inning's over. Finally.

"Why were you playing so shallow?" Chas says to me.

I feel like smacking him. "It was a gamble," I say.

"It cost us two runs."

"Sometimes you guess wrong," Emmett says.

I triple to left center to lead off the third. Nate smacks a long fly ball for an out; I tag up and score easily. The game's tied. Mike gives me a big smile.

Emmett strikes out looking, and Grady bounces out to the second baseman. Sid gets the Cubs 1-2-3 in their half.

Top of the fourth. We have two runs in, two outs.

The umpire calls a strike on Sid although the catcher catches it on the bounce. Sid gives the ump a look, then smashes the next pitch down the third-base line. He's halfway to first when the ball lands on the outfield grass and the ump calls "Foul ball!" Sid shuffles back to the plate, eyeing the ump, who ignores him.

The next pitch is below Sid's knees. "Strike!" the ump says. Sid turns to glare at the ump, who is studying the counter in the palm of his hand. He looks up to see Sid still standing there. "You're out," he says.

I look at Mike. She's not saying anything, just looking up at the sky, as if she's asking for a second opinion. She doesn't get one.

Sid stomps back to the dugout. His face is red; I can see his lips moving. "Bad call," I say to him. He slams his bat back into the rack and slumps down at the far end of the bench. Emmett goes down to talk to him, but I don't stick around to listen. I've got some pitching to do, a 6-4 lead to protect, jitters that almost take my breath away.

I start for the mound, but Mike puts her arm around my shoulders and stops me just outside the dugout. "Just play catch with Emmett," she says. "Don't worry about the batter."

"Okay." I head for the mound again.

"Nelson," she says to my back. I turn and she's coming out of the dugout grinning, my glove in her hand. "You'll need this," she says.

My nerves calm down as I throw my warmup tosses.

"Batter up!" the ump growls.

I scuff around the mound, talking to myself, before I look toward home: a little batter, a little strike zone. I was hoping for someone tall, with arms like spaghetti.

I take a deep breath, go into my windup, and release, staring at Emmett's mitt. He has to come out of his crouch to catch it. The next one's closer, but still high. I ease off on the next pitch. It floats over the plate and the guy smacks it into left for a single.

Mike comes out. "You're close, Nelson," she says, "but it looks like you're trying to aim it. Just throw it to Emmett and let the batter worry about where it is. Okay?"

I nod.

This batter is bigger, and a lefty, but I'm concentrating on Emmett. My first pitch is outside, but it feels better. I throw—faster. The batter backs away as the ball whacks into the mitt a hair inside. Emmett fires to second. Nobody's covering the base. The runner goes to third. I get two strikes on the batter before he grounds one into left. The runner scores. I begin to wish Sid could come back in.

Emmett calls time and jogs to the mound. "You're doing good, Nelson," he says. "We can afford a couple of walks. Break out your heater. Let 'em see what you've got." He heads for the plate. "Knock me over," he says over his shoulder.

The next guy up is tall and thin, with long, skinny arms and pants that are too short. I peer in at Emmett, but I see an old rotting stump on a riverbank, surrounded by pockmarked mud and jagged chunks of red wood.

I throw. The ball hums toward the plate, a low-flying cannonball. The ball thuds into Emmett's mitt, tipping him back a bit before he catches himself.

"Strike!" the ump grunts.

Emmett gives me a thumbs up and tosses the ball back. I throw two more strikes. One out. I'm feeling pumped, I'm feeling strong, I'm feeling like I belong.

I walk the next batter, but strike out the next two. The inning's over. We're still up by one. I get a hand when we return to the dugout. Chas smiles,

Sid looks relieved. My mom looks relieved.

Top of the fifth. I line out to the pitcher. Nate reaches first on an error. The first pitch to Emmett is high, and Nate goes to second. Emmett takes another pitch, low this time. "Strike!" the ump says. Sid makes a noise; Mike looks to the sky. Nate beats the throw to third.

Emmett pops a little spinner out in front of the plate. The catcher rushes out to get it. He gets his glove on the ball, but it squibs away and bounces across the line into foul territory. Emmett sprints past first base; Nate thunders across the plate.

"Foul ball!" the ump yells, and holds his arms in the air.

Our bench is on their feet, making noise. No one can believe it. If their catcher touches it in fair territory before it goes foul, it's a fair ball.

I look at Mike; she's gazing up at the heavens again. "Tell the ump," I say to her. "Tell him the catcher touched the ball."

"He's not going to change his mind, Nelson. We'll have to live with it."

"Or die with it," Chas says.

Nate goes back to third, Emmett to the plate, where

he gives the ump a look that could melt a glacier, then swings hard at the next pitch and misses. Strike three. Grady hits a soft liner to the second baseman for the third out. Our lead is still one run.

Their first batter comes to the plate, but it's just me and Emmett, playing catch. I rear back and throw heat over the inside corner.

"Strike!" the ump says.

The next pitch is a little low. "Strike!" the ump says.

I wind up and throw another heater and it pops into Emmett's mitt. "Strike!"

I've got my rhythm now. I think of the messages, of A.K. Did he know it would be like this?

The next two guys go down swinging. I hear a lot of good stuff when I get to the dugout, but there's still another inning to go.

Top of the sixth. We load the bases to start the inning. Then Woody whips his short arms through a fat pitch and blasts a line drive down the third-base line.

"Fair ball!" the ump yells. While their left fielder chases it down, Webb scores, Kevin scores, Emmett sends Hugh home. He beats the throw. We start a chant in the dugout, and it spreads to the stands: "Woo-dy! Woo-dy! Woo-dy!"

Sid singles. Woody scores. On the first pitch to me, a ball, Sid steals second. The Cubs' manager comes out. They change pitchers.

On the first pitch from the new pitcher, Sid heads for third, and slides. From halfway up the line the ump yells, "Safe!"

"He was out, ump!" The voice, a man's, loud, coming from the Cubs' bleachers, sounds familiar. The ump looks. No one's making himself obvious, but the Cubs' parents in the stands are turning around and looking at a man sitting on the end of the top row by himself. He's wearing a baseball hat and sunglasses and studying a newspaper, but I don't have a problem recognizing him: Mr. Conger. Scouting us for the Expos?

As Sid dusts himself off, as the ump glares, as everyone in the Cubs' crowd cranes their necks to look, Mr. Conger gets up, climbs down the bleachers, and leaves.

I pop the next pitch deep to left. The left fielder makes the catch, and Emmett sends Sid home. Nate and Emmett ground out, but we're ahead by six runs.

Bottom of the sixth. I strike out the first two batters. One to go, and we're in the playoffs.

I look at the stands, at the dugout, around the field. I listen: lots of chatter going on, most of it aimed at me, but I can't get distracted. Just a riverbank, just a stump. Just a guy with a bat in his hands standing next to the stump. He swings at a 1 and 2 pitch. The ball jumps off his bat, flying for center field, deep. But Grady's on the run; he tracks it down and makes a nice catch.

We celebrate on the mound, all of us, Mike, too— just one of the guys. We're in the playoffs; maybe Mr. Conger will get a chance to see us again. Maybe we'll get another chance to show him what kind of team we are now. Maybe I'll get a chance to stand on that mound, to crouch at that plate, and make a difference.

That evening I send my dad an e-mail giving him the details of our win. I end the letter with my own message: "The view from the mound is awesome."

— 1 4 —
On Watch

Thursday night Mike calls us with our playoff schedule. Our first game is Saturday at noon against the Rockies. If we win that one, we play in the championship game on Tuesday against the winner of Saturday's Expos-Marlins game.

"You pitched a great game today," she says.

"I loved pitching," I say. "Can I go against the Expos? My dad's coming home on Sunday. I've got to be able to show him I can pitch."

"We'll just have to get past the Rockies."

"Yeah." I remember the messages. "Who wrote them, Mike?"

"You tell me."

I have to find out. I have to find out who believed I could be a pitcher, who thought Mike could get our bats working, who brought our team to where we are. And with maybe only one more practice, I'm running out of chances.

*

My mom sends me to bed at nine-thirty. I hear her walk down the hall to her bedroom. I turn on my lamp, sit up on the edge of my bed, and open a book. I need to stay awake until she's asleep.

At ten I tiptoe down the hall. My mom's light's still on. I try again at ten-thirty. No light this time. I listen, hoping to pick up the sounds of steady breathing, but all I hear—or feel, really—is the sound of my own heart. *Don't go*, it says. *Don't go, don't go, don't go.*

But I have to go; I have an appointment. I get dressed and get my stuff. Without a sound, I make it down to the kitchen, where I fill a water bottle and put a banana, orange, and candy bar in a paper sack. I head out the back door and around to the front, sticking to the shadows. It's all the way dark now, but my eyes are used to it.

I adjust the sleeping bag under my arm and take off

on foot. My bike would be faster, but I can hide better if I'm walking.

A couple of cars pass, but I see them coming and get out of sight. When I get to the park entrance I head for the baseball field. A faint breeze swirls across the diamond, stirring up the finest particles of dirt. Chas's message—trampled and smeared—is still there. I'm not too late.

I walk toward the cedars. The lamp behind the backstop glows dim, throwing a circle of weak yellow light onto the infield. It's darker in the trees, but I know where I'm going.

"Gannon?" I say. My voice comes out loud.

Near the big cedar a flashlight, pointed in my direction, flickers on, off, on, off. "I am the ghost of Andy Kirk," a voice says, drawing out each syllable. "You have come uninvited to my home. Identify yourself…or die!"

"It's me," I say. "And I think he's not that kind of ghost."

Gannon's waiting for me behind the big cedar with his flashlight back on and pointed up from underneath his chin to make himself look scary. He doesn't look scary; he looks like a kid with a flashlight under his chin.

"What took you so long?" he says in his regular voice.

I explain about my mom holding me up. Then I locate a perfect place for my sleeping bag—a kind of valley between two root ridges. Gannon's bag is laid out one thick root away, with a small backpack next to it. From here we can see the field without being seen. I sit down on my bag. I can smell the tree, the grass, and the dirt. I comb my fingers through the soft grass, thinking about those five missing coins.

The night has turned chilly. We crawl inside our bags, our backs against the cedar, listening to the sounds of wind sifting through the upper branches of the tree. "Thanks for coming," I say. I'm not sure I'd want to spend the night here alone.

"No problem," Gannon says. "I'm as curious as you are."

"What if your dad finds out you snuck out of the house?"

Gannon forces a little laugh. "Son," he says, trying to mimic his dad's voice, "I thought we had an understanding, but if you feel you're old enough to sneak out of the house, lose your precious sleep, camp out in the park all night, and scare your mother and me to death, it's okay by me."

"Yeah, right," I say.

"He'd kill me," Gannon says, and something in his real-life voice makes me think he believes it. Not kill, exactly, but maybe make him wish he were dead.

What would it be like to have a dad like that? Suddenly I'm thankful for mine, even if he isn't around all the time, even if the only way we talk is by e-mail.

We stare out at the field, waiting silently. When will he come? From where? For a living, breathing person the entrance is the easiest, but there are lots of ways into the park: the trees straight across the field, our left, our right, behind us. And a ghost? A ghost could drop from the big cedar like a spider on a thread of web, unseen, to scribble his message in the dirt.

I fight to stay awake, downing the orange, then the banana. Gannon eats some kind of healthy trail mix his dad invented. We talk about baseball and school, but mostly about possibilities, about who might be writing the messages. Our voices drop to whispers. I save the candy bar, with its crinkly, noisy wrapping, for later.

The breeze has died. Dead quiet settles on the park. Nothing is happening on the field, where a misty halo hangs around the light.

I take one more look at the diamond, at the alarm

setting on my watch, and close my eyes. School tomorrow. Practice tomorrow.

Something wakes me. I have the sense of someone murmuring—high in the tree—but then it's gone. Something—some urge—pulls me to my feet. As if in a trance, I find myself spreading my arms wide across the trunk, looking up, listening but not hearing. I breathe in the cedar's perfumy heat and let go.

I turn my flashlight on Gannon. He's snoozing, his sleeping bag rising and falling with each quiet breath. I slide back into my bag and close my eyes.

I doze.

I wake up again, wondering: what just happened? A dream? Maybe, but it seemed real.

Something catches my eye. I swear I see a light near the entrance to the park, but then it's gone. I ease out of my sleeping bag and stand, waiting for the light to come back on. *It does.* Just for an instant. About halfway in on the right field grass. And now I can see a shape, moving toward the infield, somebody bent over a bike. I poke Gannon awake, and he sits up, rubbing his eyes.

"Shhh!" I whisper before he can say anything. "Someone's coming." He leans forward and stares.

From out of the murk a figure emerges, moving

toward home plate. The guy stops at the message place and studies the ground. I expect him to start writing. Instead, he walks around the area for a minute, then pushes the bike away from the plate.

Toward us. I freeze while he makes his way around the fence and past the benches. He passes close to the circle of light, but not close enough for me to see his face. And now he's coming into the shadows, closer. Gannon sheds his bag and crouches beside me.

The guy is twenty feet away when I turn on my flashlight and point it at him. His hands fly up, his bike falls over. I have no trouble recognizing the face: it belongs to Chas.

I turn the flashlight on my face, then on Gannon, standing next to me now.

"Nelson! Gannon!"

"What was it going to be this time?" I say. "'Don't ever take Chas out of the game'?"

"Nothing. It was going to be nothing. What are you guys doing here?"

"We're waiting for the message man," Gannon says. "Instead we end up with the forger."

"I came to find out who it is, too. You sure it's not one of you?" He looks at Gannon, then me. "I didn't think about it before, but Gannon could be doing it."

Gannon laughs. "I didn't even know about the messages until yesterday."

I point the flashlight at our sleeping bags. "We wouldn't need to stay all night just to write a message."

"Me, neither." Chas switches on his flashlight and waves it at his bike. A sleeping bag is tied to a rack behind the seat. He picks up his bike, wheels it over, and unrolls his bag next to mine in another hollow between root ridges. "Any ideas?" he says to me.

"Not really. If you don't count you and me, there's eight possibilities. Plus Mike, if you want to include her. I wouldn't."

"Why not?" Gannon says. "Some of the messages don't sound like a kid wrote 'em."

I think about what my dad said. "If she wanted to tell us something, she'd just tell us," I say. "She wouldn't pretend to be a ghost."

"I don't know," Gannon says. "You guys are listening to the ghost. You might not listen to her."

I wonder if he's right. If Mike just *told* us the stuff in the messages, would we be playing as well as we are? Would Hugh and Kevin still be battling? Would I be pitching? Would Chas be out here in the dark, thinking about somebody besides himself?

We get in our sleeping bags. A thin fog has rolled in.

"I've got my watch set for three-thirty," I say. "If he hasn't come by now, I think it'll be early morning."

"Right," Chas says. I can hear Gannon's even breathing. He's already back to sleep.

I break out my candy bar and twist it in half. "Here," I say to Chas.

"Thanks," he says. He takes a bite.

The park lies quiet. Off in the distance somewhere a siren whines out and fades away. I look up at the branches, hear Chas begin to breathe slow and deep.

This time the alarm wakes me, a faint chirp. I look out at the field and see nothing. I shake Chas and Gannon, who sit up and stare out at the infield. "Nobody?" Gannon whispers.

"No sign," I say.

"Should we go look?" Chas says.

I figure it's a waste, but we climb out of our sleeping bags and start toward home plate. The air is cold, and I shiver.

Chas clicks on his flashlight first and whistles. "An early bird," he says.

Two new messages are scratched in the dirt:

UMPIRES DON'T LOSE
BALL GAMES—TEAMS DO.

DON'T LISTEN TO THE THUNDER.
LISTEN TO YOUR HEART. —AK

P.S. SWEET DREAMS?

Suddenly the air feels colder. I scrape away the question with my shoe, wondering how he found us, how long he stood over our sleeping bodies, whether he laughed out loud. Do ghosts laugh?

I concentrate on the first message and think about the ump we had in the Cubs game. How it seemed like he was against us. How we were letting him get to us.

But the second message is a puzzle. What thunder? How can you ignore it? Who should listen to his heart?

I look at Gannon in the dim light. He's staring at the ground, his mouth set in a straight-across line. Now he does look scary, like not himself. I expect him to say something—*Weird* or *Strange* or *Sneaky*—but he says nothing.

Chas looks around. "You think he's here someplace now?"

"Could be," I say.

But we don't stick around to look. We pack up and leave. I make it home unnoticed. The house is dark from the outside, quiet on the inside. I get to my room and crash.

— 15 —
A Friend

When Mike gets out of her car at practice, she gives my tired face a look. "Big game tomorrow," she says. "You guys get some sleep tonight."

I nod. She said "you guys" but I'm awake enough to know who she was talking to. We tell her about the new messages and walk to the infield with her.

She studies the writing. "They look authentic," she says, glancing at Chas. "The first one makes sense."

We mostly agree on that one; only Sid doesn't seem real sure.

"Umps make mistakes," Mike says, "but they even out eventually. So you don't really get hurt unless you let them get to you."

"What's the other one mean, Mike?" Emmett says.

Mike grins. "I was afraid one of you would ask." She stares at the ground, off at the trees, back again, as if the answer is around somewhere if you just knew where to look. "I don't know," she says finally. "Which is a good sign—for those of you who are still wondering—that I'm not writing these. The message means something to me, but it's personal. Maybe each of you needs to think of what it means to you."

I think about it but don't come up with anything. As we start practice, I see Gannon riding his bike across the outfield grass.

"Hi," Mike says as he sits down on her bench. She's out working with us.

"Hi," Gannon says. I wish I could see him out on the field with us, wearing his Dodgers cap, smiling, laughing. But he sits, bareheaded; he doesn't look happy.

"Bring your glove today?" Mike asks him.

"Not today," Gannon says.

"Think about batting, then," Mike says.

During batting practice Mike pitches about half the pitches to each player, with Sid and me alternating on the other half. Halfway through, Chas takes the catcher's spot.

Mike looks over at Gannon. "You ready?"

Gannon shakes his head. "Just watching," he says, but the way he says it tells me he'd like nothing better than to be standing in that batter's box. Mike senses it, too. "Come on," she says.

Gannon shrugs and gets up and walks to the plate. I half-expect some grumbling from some of the guys. Gannon's not a Dodger anymore; he's the enemy now. Why give him a chance to get even better? Why take practice time away from one of our guys? But nobody says anything. Everyone's attention is on the plate as Gannon slips on a helmet, shoulders our biggest bat, and gets into his stance. The field gets quiet.

Mike starts him off easy, and he crushes a couple of long fouls to left. She speeds it up, and he's hitting monster fly balls and line drives, fair now, to left and left-center. More speed—most of what she's got, I figure—and he's still meeting her pitches, lining some to center, hitting some on the ground, popping some up. But he's still meeting them. He has a grin on his face, but not a cocky grin. He's having fun.

"You're a hitter, Gannon," Mike says. She smiles and eyes Chas. Her arm is a blur as she windmills through her motion and releases the ball. It smacks into Chas's glove before Gannon's bat crosses the plate. He backs away, takes a practice cut, and steps back in.

Mike gives him another one—same speed, same location. He takes a big cut at it, but the ball's already in Chas's mitt.

"One more like that," Gannon says.

Mike nods, but she drops her speed a little bit—at least it looks like it to me—and Gannon connects, fouling it back. She gives him another one, and he lines it to right. "Run on the next one," she says, and throws him another near-heater. He knocks it deep to right center and makes it all the way to third before the ball catches up to him.

He walks to the mound. "Thanks for letting me hit," he says to Mike, handing her his helmet. "I should get going."

"You're welcome," Mike says. "But I didn't let you hit. You got those on your own."

"It was fun."

"Good luck tomorrow," Mike says, and shakes Gannon's hand.

"You, too," he says. He goes to his bike and rides off, turning once to wave to us. I keep my eyes on him. By the time he gets to the park entrance, he looks small.

We gather at the mound, our hands joined in a knot in the middle of the circle.

"Who's got a cheer?" Mike says.

"Go, Dodgers!" Sid says.

"Go, Expos!" I say. We all want a chance to play against the best. And if anyone besides us wins the playoffs, I want it to be Gannon's team.

— 16 —
The Rockies

Everybody's at North Creek Park early; everybody's put on their game face. The Rockies are good; we know that. They've beaten us twice already. But we don't want to just show up; we're planning on winning.

We're the home team, in the field first. When I take the mound, I feel loose. I begin with some easy warmup tosses, just targeting Sid's glove, then gradually increase the speed until the leather pops, the dust rises, Sid smiles. Some of the Rockies are standing in front of their dugout, looking at me and talking. One guy points at me. I wonder if something's wrong with my uniform. I check; my jersey's on frontwards, I'm wearing my pants.

The Rockies all go to a different school, and with their helmets on, they look pretty much the same. I don't remember the first batter from last time, but I just throw my heater and get him looking at strike three. The next guy hits one down the first-base line. Kevin makes a nice stop and steps on the bag. The third kid goes down trying to catch up with a stump-buster down the heart of the plate.

I start for our dugout, but their last batter's walking toward the mound, trying to get my attention. I stop.

"We thought you left the Dodgers," he says.

I don't get it at first. Then I do. "*Gannon* left. He's on the Expos now."

He looks at my face as if he doesn't believe me. I take off my cap, show him my blond hair. "Who are you?" he says.

"My name's Nelson."

I go back to the dugout, at least a couple of feet off the ground. The guy thought I was *the Cannon*.

"They thought I was Gannon," I tell our guys.

They laugh and high-five me and pull the cap off my head and mess up my hair.

"They thought he was Gannon," Emmett says,

shaking his head and grinning.

"Way to look out there, Nelson," Mike says, and gives me a half-hug.

Grady, Webb, and Kevin go down in order, but at least they all make contact with the ball. Last time against the Rockies we were waving at a lot of strikes, or standing and watching them go by.

I walk the first batter on four pitches wide of the plate. The next guy's a lefty. My first pitch is outside. Sid comes to the mound.

"You're outside, outside, outside, Nelson," he says. "Forget the batters. You're not gonna hurt 'em. Throw it to me."

"I'm trying."

"Play ball!" the ump yells.

I get the next two guys on strikes, but the runner, on third now, comes home on an error by Hugh. The next batter knocks one past Hugh, and another run scores.

I decide to go inside, to move the batter back. I throw, trying for the corner, but the ball gets away from me and ends up a foot inside and high, zipping past his chin. The guy backs up. I go inside again, and he bails out. The count is 2 and 0, but he's standing at the edge of the batter's box. The guys are talking behind me, telling me to throw easy, to just throw strikes. I hear Mike's voice. "See the target, Nelson," she says.

I see the target; I get him on two called strikes and one he goes for.

Hugh singles to start us out, but Woody lines one to the pitcher, who turns and throws to first for a double play. Sid smashes a triple.

I start out of the dugout, but Grady stops me and hands me his Easton, the bat I've been admiring all season. "Crunch one for us," he says.

I step to the plate, checking my setup, fingering the shiny bat.

The first pitch is outside, but not by much, and I almost go for it. "Strike!" the ump says. I take a deep breath, tap the plate, stare out at the pitcher through the rising dust. I've got to go for anything close.

The second pitch looks outside again, but I swing and watch the ball rocket over the second baseman's head. I cruise into first. Sid scores.

I steal second, then third, on the first two pitches to Nate. He grounds the next one into left. I jog home. Chas pops out, but we've tied the game, 2-2.

Top of three. Emmett comes in at catcher, Sid goes

to right, Woody to the bench. My last inning to pitch. The first guy walks, but then it's force out, strike out, pop out.

We get another run in the bottom of the third to take the lead.

Sid's pitching to start the fourth, I'm in the dugout with Mike. Her ponytail whips side to side as she paces back and forth. I stand with my face up against the dugout fence, but my feet want to move, I want to be on the field.

"Where am I next?" I ask Mike.

"Center. We need a strong arm out there."

The Rockies go down in order. Sid leads off for us by grounding out, and Woody strikes out. Nate gets to first on an error, but Chas hits into a force to end the inning.

Top of the fifth. Still 3-2. I go to center, Grady goes to the bench. They get a guy on third with one out. The next batter launches a high fly ball toward left. Chas chases it down and makes the catch. The runner tags and goes. Chas throws, and Emmett sets himself in front of the plate.

It all happens in an instant: Emmett stretching high to catch the ball, the runner sliding into home and undercutting him, Emmett crashing down with the ball in his mitt, twisting in the air to try to make the tag but landing on the back of his head on the dirt.

The ump spreads his arms, his hands flat above the ground. "Safe!"

The runner stands and wobbles to the dugout. Emmett's on the ground, not moving. Mike runs out; Emmett's parents come to the backstop and press their faces to the fence. Mike and the umpire crouch over Emmett, the Rockies' manager comes over, all of us inch closer.

Mike gets Emmett to sit up, gets some ice to the back of his head. She and the ump talk to him. I see her hold up two fingers, then one, in front of his face. They get him to his feet, take off his catcher's gear. It lies in the dirt as Mike helps him to the dugout. His mom and dad join him. We give him a cheer. I'm glad he's able to walk, at least. But who's going to play catcher?

Mike talks to Emmett and his parents for a minute, then comes out of the dugout. "Chas!" she calls, and waves him in.

Mike sends Grady to left, and while Chas gets on his gear, Emmett heads for the parking lot with his folks. Everyone on both sides gives him a hand.

Chas, nervously popping his bare fist into the catcher's mitt, squats behind the plate and takes some tosses from Sid.

The next batter swings at the first pitch but misses, and the ball gets past Chas and all the way to the backstop.

"Keep it in front of you, Chas," Mike says.

The next pitch is a ball, and Chas hangs on. Another swing and a miss on the next one. Chas drops the ball, but gets his knees down and blocks it. Sid throws one outside and low, but the guy goes for it and taps it right back to the mound. He's out before he's halfway to first. Easy, but the Rockies have a run back. It's 3-3.

Bottom of the fifth. I walk to start the inning. Webb pops out. Kevin walks. Hugh triples to right, scoring me and Kevin. We're ahead, 5-3. The noise level rises to earsplitting in the dugout as Kevin leads us in a chant of Hugh's name. Hugh tries to come home on a passed ball, but gets thrown out. Grady lines the next pitch to the left fielder.

Top of the sixth. If we can hold the lead, we're in the championship. Just outside the dugout we all gather in a tight circle, hands knotted, and Mike tells us that Emmett could have a concussion, that he's gone to the hospital. "Let's give him a shout," she says. We count to three and yell his name so loud that I figure if he's still in Snohomish County somewhere, he hears us.

The first batter singles, steals second, and goes to third on a dribbler that nobody handles.

Sid walks the next batter. The bases are loaded and nobody's out.

"Force at home!" Webb says. "Force everywhere!"

The next guy powders one toward me. Halfway there, I know I'm not going to get it, but the Rockies don't know that. If I can decoy my catch till the last second, I can hold them on base. I keep my eyes on the ball, reaching my glove out in front of me like a basket.

I snag the ball on the first bounce and fire the ball to Webb at second, forcing out the runner who was trapped on first. But the runner on third scores, the runner on second moves to third, and the batter's safe at first.

"Play's at home," Webb tells the infield.

"Play's at home," I tell Grady and Woody, but with Chas at catcher, what chance do we have to get the runner?

The batter hits a sharp grounder under Sid's glove. I charge, but before the ball gets past second, Webb scoops it up, sets his feet, and fires home. Chas is there, waiting, as the runner thunders in from third, as the ball flies. *Catch it*, I pray. *Catch it.*

He does. He catches Webb's perfect throw—knee-high, a couple of feet up the third-base line—and pivots to greet the runner, who hits the dirt. Chas gets the mitt down and makes the tag before the runner's slide takes him across home plate. They collide, but when Chas bounces to his feet, he's holding his mitt high. The ball is in it.

"Out!" the ump says. Two outs. Guys on first and third.

"Great play, Webb!" Mike yells. "Great play, Chas!"

Our fans are standing and cheering. But we need another out.

Sid throws a bullet, right down the middle of the plate. The batter swings, and the ball arches up into the blue sky, toward me. I take a step back, but the ball seems to hang up there in the wind like a small white bird.

The ball starts down, and I stare at it, concentrating, knees bent, ready to adjust if I have to. But I don't. The ball pops into my glove and I squeeze it tight. We've won. We're in the championship game. I take off running for the mound as the guys come together there, chesting into one another, clinging and tussling like puppies. I look beyond, to the stands, and imagine my dad, standing tall, smiling.

Homecomings

Emmett doesn't have a concussion—just a headache and a sore neck. His mom and dad take him and me out for pizza that night to celebrate our victory, and I give him a play-by-play of the last two innings. Meanwhile, my mom's home, getting ready for my dad's arrival. We're going to the airport the next morning to meet him. I'm too excited to eat much pizza.

When I get home, Mike calls: the Expos won their game. We're playing them for the championship. I go to bed early, but I have a hard time falling asleep. I keep thinking: *Second chances are as rare as rainbows.* I try to remember the last time I saw a rainbow; I can't. I know we'll only have one chance to play the Expos.

Before we leave for the airport in the morning, I study the picture of my dad. My memory of his face has gotten fuzzy since he's been gone.

But when he gets off the plane, everything about him is the same as always—the way he sounds, the way his arms go around us, his smell, the feel of his stubble against my cheek. He slips into the back seat behind my mom. So he can look at both of us, he says, but he closes his eyes, breathes deep, and sinks down in the upholstery. I sit next to him and hold his hand.

I know he's tired, so on the way home I give him just a short update on the Rockies game, my pitching and hitting, how all the guys keep improving. He livens up, but his eyes look half-sad. "I wish I could have been here to see it all," he says.

"Me, too," I say.

He looks at me. "You still haven't figured out who's writing the messages?"

My mom shakes her head.

"One person knows, I guess," I say.

"Right. Unless the writer really is Andy Kirk's ghost," my dad says.

I look to see if he's smiling. He's not.

"Has anybody tried to find out who it is?" he says.

I try to look innocent. "Not that I know of."

"Man, if it were my team I'd be sneaking over to the park in the middle of the night to see if I could catch the guy."

I keep a straight face. "Really?"

"Don't give him any ideas, Greg," my mom says.

My dad winks at me. "I'm glad you saved a game for me."

"The championship game," I say. "We're gonna win."

"I don't doubt it," my dad says.

*

After dinner my dad and I head to the park to play some catch. The big cedar tugs at us like a magnet, and without deciding, we walk until we're standing in its huge shadow. We circle its trunk, looking up.

"He was quite a kid, I guess," my dad says. "He meant so much to someone that they did this." He gazes up at the bare trunk, the scars. He looks around at the other scarred trees.

"And now somebody's leaving messages from him," I say.

"And people are taking them to heart," my dad says. "I'm taking one message to heart: 'Second chances are as rare as rainbows.'" He puts his arm around my shoulders and pulls me close. "There isn't going to be a second chance to see you grow up. And I've been missing out on my only one."

I don't know what to say. But something in his eyes gives me a birthday party kind of feeling—the kind you get right before it's time to open that last big present.

"Sit down," he says, and we sit right down between the root ridges where not very long ago Gannon and Chas and I spent most of a night. It's different here in the early evening—warmer, brighter, safer. "Your mom and I have already talked about this, and she's all for it, too, but I wanted to let you know what's happening."

"Something good?" I say. He's still smiling, but this is turning into one of those serious one-on-one conversations that can sometimes go bad.

His smile gets bigger. "Something good," he says. "I've been contacting people at other companies, sending out my updated résumé, looking at job opportunities—the kind that would allow me to stay right around here nearly all the time. And believe it or not, there's some real interest in your old dad."

"You wouldn't have to travel?" Now it really does feel like my birthday.

"That would be my main condition for any job I take."

"How soon?" I say, pressing my luck.

"Not long," he says. "You might just end up having me around here more than you want."

I shake my head. Not possible. I think about having him at all my games, coming to the park and playing catch whenever we want. I could take him to the river and show him my pitching spot. Maybe we'd find a new one. "We could do lots of stuff together," I say. "You could teach me everything you know about baseball."

"It sounds as if you may have already passed me up," he says. "But I'll try my best to help you."

We get up and walk toward the infield with my dad's arm around my shoulders. I step away and toss him the ball. We move out into the warm sunshine, throwing faster.

*

Monday comes quick, but I don't mind. I run into Emmett on the way to practice. Chas and Nate are already standing at the message spot, looking down at the ground, when we get within sight of the diamond. We get off our bikes and look at the newest messages:

MOVE THE WEB TO SECOND BASE WHEN
NELSON IS PITCHING. WHEN THE ROOKIE
IS IN THEIR, THE OTHER TEAMS ARE
SWINGING LATE.

PUT A SMILE ON YOUR
GAME FACE. —AK

The spelling thing again—*their* instead of *there* this time. I think back to the Rockies game. They *were* hitting my stuff to the right side; Hugh had a few problems handling it. But Webb sucks up everything hit anywhere near him.

The rest of the guys show up. Some of them don't like the message. Everything's going good; why mess with it? Others, including me, are for it. But no one wants to hurt Hugh's feelings, or make Sid think he doesn't throw as hard as I do. I keep my mouth shut and wait for Mike.

"Whoever wrote this message is doing some thinking," Mike says when she gets there. "As far as the infield change goes, that's for you guys to decide. And I think Hugh and Webb should have the most say."

"If Hugh's okay with it, I am," Webb says.

"I know how to play shortstop," Hugh says. "I've been watching Webb all season."

"It's okay with you?" Mike asks Hugh.

He smiles. "It's great."

"It takes ten," Emmett says.

Halfway through batting practice, we all turn to look as an old man heads from the parking lot toward us.

"Don't mind me, kids," he says when he gets closer. I like his voice. It floats to us effortlessly, but it's soft and friendly. "Just carry on with your practice."

We don't. We watch as he continues on toward the trees. He reaches the big cedar and stops in its wide shadow. He looks up, as if searching for something. He circles the tree, then stops, lays his hand on the bark, and bends close. Except for the sound of a bird or two, the park is silent. The whole team is standing near home plate now, eyes on the man.

Finally, he stands tall, gives the tree a pat, and walks toward us. "Don't let me bother you, folks," he says. "I'd like to see some good ball while I'm here."

"A scout," Chas says, grinning.

"Mr. Kirk?" Mike says. The name sends a tickle down my spine. For just a second I'm thinking *Andy*, but it can't be. This man is no ghost.

"That's right," he says. "Do I know you?"

"I don't think so," she says. "My team was practicing here a few years ago—this place was just grass and trees then—when you came to the park. My manager—Mr. Harris—knew you."

"I remember that."

"Would you mind coming over here for a minute, Mr. Kirk?" Mike says.

"Not at all." He makes his way from behind the fence and toward the plate. He's somewhere in his seventies, I figure, but he walks younger—big stride, arms swinging. "Want me to throw some batting practice?" he says, grinning.

"Sure," Mike says. "But I want to show you something." Mike shows him what's left of the message. We take turns telling him about the others.

"My turn now?" he says finally.

We say yes.

"First, my name's Sam Kirk—the Sam Kirk mentioned in the newspaper article some of you saw. I'm Andy Kirk's older brother. Ten years older, actually—old enough to go to war during World War II. Everybody worried about me making it back home, but nobody worried about Andy. He was way too young to go. Then he ends up falling out of a tree and dying." He looks around the park. "Even the trees suffered. But you've heard the story. I live in Minnesota now, but I come back every few years about this time and pay a visit.

"There's been some odd things happening in this park since Andy's death, but mysterious notes written in the dirt? Not that I recall. For a long time there wasn't even any dirt here." His eyes smile as he looks around at the circle of faces. "Maybe one of you has the secret."

"Did he like baseball?" Chas asks.

"Lived for it. To Andy, baseball was almost like a religion—a sacred thing. He studied the game, players, teams, statistics. He loved to play, and he practiced every chance he could get, even during the long rainy winters we had up here. He was always dragging me out in the cold to play catch or work on his batting, and when I was gone to war, I think he about wore out our dad's arm. Andy had this dream of playing in the big leagues someday, and I like to think he would have done it. He had an arm like a slingshot and a quick bat. And that big league attitude: always play your hardest, play for the good of the team, don't even think about cheating, treat your opponents with respect."

"He liked to watch, too?" Emmett says.

"If he wasn't playing, he'd be watching," Sam says. "That's why he was up in that old cedar that day, watching his big brother, keeping score of the game. He had this habit—a system, he called it—of using coins to keep track of the score. You fellas ever find any old nickels or pennies under the big cedar, they could be Andy's."

So my dad's story is true. I imagine discovering the coins, dirty and discolored, beneath a small but ancient shrub.

"I often wonder what would have happened if I'd struck out on that last at-bat instead of hitting that dinger," Sam Kirk says. "Silly, I guess, but I can't help myself. It's natural to look for someone—or something—to blame." He smiles, but I see some sadness in his eyes. More than a half-century later, there's still some sadness in his eyes.

I take a deep breath. "Was he good in school—a good speller?"

"He was pretty good in school, as I remember. Like most kids his age, he'd rather have been doing something else."

"Does this writing look like his?" Mike says.

He shakes his head. "I can't really say. But I can't say

it's not like his writing. I can't say that." He grins, big and broad, and squints at a big white cloud passing close to the sun. "What if it were?"

"Who cut off the branches?" Sid says, getting away from the subject of ghosts.

Sam Kirk smiles. "Some things need to be left unsaid. I will tell you one thing: before I went into the army, I worked summers at a logging camp. I got to be pretty good with a saw. But me and the old tree—we made our peace a long time ago."

We don't ask Sam Kirk any more questions. He tosses a few easy pitches to Nate, but he looks like he could still throw it hard. He watches from the bench as we continue batting practice.

When it's my turn, Sid pitches to me first, then Mike takes over. She starts off slow, but quickly heats it up. I hit the first three well. I dig in, expecting her heater next, but it's a slow change-up. I almost commit, but don't, and when the ball crosses the plate I've got it timed just right. I blast it deep to left, over Chas's head.

I'm fighting down a rising feeling of excitement in my chest. I feel like I've arrived somewhere special, and I don't want to leave, ever. I dig in again, expecting the big pitch, and this time it comes. I stare at the blur and swing, getting my bat on the ball and knocking it over Webb's head into right field.

Mike gives me the thumbs-up sign.

"The heater?" I say.

"None other. Congratulations, Nelson."

I don't fight the feeling anymore. I let it come, I let it rise up and swell my throat and bring tears to my eyes. I wanted to be a pitcher, and I am, but Mike's let me be a hitter, too.

When practice ends we have a huddle on the mound, where we come up with a cheer: "Andy Kirk!" We invite Sam Kirk to our game, and he says he'll try to be there.

I ride away from the field with Emmett, Chas, and Sid, but nobody says much. I'm thinking about the game. I'm thinking I'm ready.

— 18 —
The Expos

Tuesday. Game day. I sit in school, frowning at the clock as the hands creep around its face. Mrs. King, our teacher, is talking, but her words are wasted on me. I'm focused on one thing: the game. Finally, the bell rings.

Mike wants us at North Creek Park at five o'clock for the six o'clock game. We're all there before five. Fourteen Expos are taking infield practice on the diamond next to us. Gannon's at first. If he starts there, we'll see Trey Holcumb on the mound in the first inning. Not much difference. He's bigger than Gannon and throws rockets.

Their bleachers are full. Raymond's mom sits next to his dad, who's sitting next to Gannon's mom. Next to her sits Mr. Conger, elbows on his knees, chin on his hands, staring out at us. I get a dry, heavy feeling in my stomach, as if I've just slid into second headfirst and swallowed a pound of dirt.

Sid and I go with Emmett and Chas to the left-field fence to warm up. Sid's the starting pitcher; I'm in center. I won't be pitching for more than an hour.

The outfield grass is freshly mowed; its sweet smell fills my nose, its green streaks the white hides of balls that come in too low or sail out of reach. When Mike calls us in, I rake my fingers through the blades of grass and carry their scent back to the third-base dugout. Our bleachers are crammed. Sam Kirk is sitting next to my mom. He's wearing a Dodgers cap. I scan the rest of the crowd, almost disappointed when I don't spot a round-faced, smiling kid dressed in old-fashioned clothes and a vintage baseball cap, fingering a stack of coins.

There's a lot of noise, but I pick out a familiar voice from the rest as it cheers on the guys one by one. "Easy does it, Sid," my dad says at the end of his roll call. "One-two-three."

The first batter walks and steals second on a strike-out. Trey Holcumb singles. The runner scores. Gannon walks to the plate. He exchanges nods with Sid, then digs in. I hear Mr. Conger's voice, rising above the others. "No pitcher, Gannon!" he yells. "Rag arm, Gannon! Be a hitter!"

I look at Sid's parents. His mom is staring toward the Expos bleachers and shaking her head. His dad's face is red.

"You're the guy, Sid baby," Mike says. "Just see Emmett. Just hit that old mitt."

Sid throws. He's got some heat on it, and it pops into Emmett's mitt for a strike.

"Be a hitter, son!" Mr. Conger growls.

Sid's next pitch is outside, but Gannon swings anyway and misses. The ball gets away from Emmett. Trey goes to second.

"Wait for your pitch, Gannon," Mr. Conger says. The noise from the other parents has died to a murmur, and his voice carries like a message from the heavens. Or somewhere else. I wonder how Gannon is supposed to decide. Be a hitter? Wait for your pitch? Part of me wants Gannon to do something good, even if it hurts us, so his dad will get off his back.

Sid sneaks one over the outside corner for strike three. Gannon walks back to the dugout looking into the stands, where his dad stands up, whips his cap off his head and slaps it against his thigh.

The next batter grounds out. The guys come back to the dugout, patting Sid on the back. We've faced some big hitters and given up only one run.

Trey warms up on the mound. Mike calls us all together. "This guy's fast. I hear Gannon is, too. Remember what we've been working on in batting practice. You guys can hit fast pitching. Just go up there ready to swing, and set up at the back of the batter's box. You'll get a little more time. Okay?"

We say okay.

Mike gives Sid a knock on the helmet. "Go get 'em, Sid."

Sid smacks the second pitch into right for a single. Woody and Grady go out to coach the bases, I start for the plate.

Mike stops me. "You can hit this guy, Nelson. Wait for something close, then punish it. If it's not close, let it go, and we'll see if Sid can take second on his own."

I set myself at the back of the box.

"Easy out, Trey!" Mr. Conger booms.

I dig in. I'll show him. I swing hard at the first pitch, but it's high and outside and I miss it badly. Still, Sid steals second.

Trey's next two pitches are outside. He thinks he has a sucker. I lay off. Finally he throws one down the middle. I take my cut and feel the bat on the ball, solid. It flies over the third baseman's head.

"Go!" Woody says as I dig for second. The throw goes to the plate, and I get to third. I look toward home, where the ump has his hands spread wide. Sid jumps to his feet and flashes me the thumbs-up sign. The game is tied. I hear my name as our players and fans get loud.

The Expos are quiet. I look toward their bleachers. Mr. Conger is gone. I see him outside the fence near first base, talking to Gannon. Gannon's saying nothing. He nods, but his face is blank.

I score on Nate's fly ball to center, putting us ahead, 2-1, but Chas goes down swinging, and Webb lines out on an all-star, diving grab by Gannon.

"Great catch, Gannon," Mike yells. He gets up, dusting himself off, looking puzzled, then grinning at Mike. I haven't seen his grin for a while.

The Expos go down 1-2-3 in the second. Hugh

gets a walk in our half of the inning, but that's it.

Top of the third. Sid gets Raymond looking at a chest-high fastball for strike three. Mr. Conger gets on the ump, who goes over and says something to him through the fence. The ump talks to the Expos' manager and returns to the plate. Mr. Conger shuts up.

The next batter hits a sharp grounder to third. Grady boots it, and the Expos have a runner on first.

Trey beats out a perfect bunt up the first-base line.

Gannon's up. Sid's careful with him—too careful. He walks him on four pitches to load the bases. He follows that with a strikeout, but the next batter singles, driving in two runs. Webb makes a nice play on a grounder for the final out. We're down, 3-2.

"We've kept it close," Mike says in the dugout. "Now it's our turn."

Sid draws a walk and steals second on a ball to me. The next pitch is exactly what I'm looking for: belt-high and down the middle. I drive it over Sid's head. He scores. But I'm stranded at second when Grady, Chas, and Webb go down in order.

Top of the fourth. Hugh moves to shortstop, Webb to second, Nate to center, Sid to the bench. I'm pitching. *I'm pitching.* Mike pulls me aside while Emmett

pulls on his gear. I hear my name from the bleachers—
Sid's dad's voice, my mom's. My dad's. I look up at him
through the dugout fence. He's grinning, big.

"I want you to relax out there, Nelson," Mike says.
Sweat trickles down from under my chin; I have to tell
myself to breathe. I nod. "If you're not having a good
time, what's the point?"

"I see *you* pacing."

"It's the manager's job to pace. It's your job to play
the game."

My first pitch drifts outside for ball one. I take a
breath. I stare at Emmett's mitt and throw. Strike, at
the knees—a good pitch.

"Attaway, Nelson baby," Emmett says, and the
other guys chime in. I throw again—harder—and the
batter swings and misses, but he hasn't seen my heat
yet. I wind up and throw the fastball and he swings—
late—and gets nothing but air. I want to jump in the air,
I want to yell, but it's only one out. Eight—at least—to
go.

I walk the next batter, then whip my heater past
Raymond for strike three. The base runner steals second. I start worrying about him and give up another
walk. Guys on first and second and Trey coming to bat.

Not the start I'd imagined. But I bear down, and get Trey to hit a little roller right back to me off an outside pitch at the knees. I throw him out easily at first base.

Kevin gets on his helmet as the Cannon warms up. We all knew he'd pitch this game; I was hoping it wouldn't happen until later, with us way ahead, when it wouldn't matter what we did against our friend. But there he is, fourth inning, score tied, cap tipped back on his head, throwing smoke. Even in warmups, he's throwing smoke.

"Back of the box, Kevin," Mike says. "Way back," she says under her breath.

Kevin steps to the plate. He's faced Gannon before, but only in practice, only at half-speed. He looks nervous.

Gannon goes with the fastball on the first pitch. But Kevin doesn't back off. He takes a cut and gets a piece of it, fouling it into the backstop.

"Smoke him, Gannon." Mr. Conger's voice pours out of the stands like swamp water; I can almost smell it.

But Kevin looks more confident as Gannon delivers. It's outside, and Kevin holds up.

"Smoke him, Gannon," Mr. Conger says. The voice sounds like a recording.

Gannon throws another fastball, but Kevin's ready with a quick, compact swing. He drives the ball into right field and stands on first, grinning.

Gannon stares over at first as if he can't believe Kevin's there, then strikes out Hugh on three pitches. Kevin steals second. Emmett goes down swinging. Woody hits a dribbler back to Gannon, who throws to first. It's on target, but the first baseman bobbles it. Woody's safe. Kevin goes to third.

Gannon throws Nate an off-speed pitch. He lines it into center for a single. Kevin scores easily, Woody gets to third. We're ahead, 4-3.

Our dugout goes wild. I walk to the plate for my first at-bat against the Cannon, expecting Mr. Conger to say something. He doesn't. Maybe he thinks I'm not worth it. I want to show him I am. I watch Gannon fidget with the ball before he looks in and pitches.

"Strike!" the ump says. I dig in, vowing to swing at the next one if it's close. It is. I swing and just barely make contact. The ball glances back to the backstop.

Now I'm expecting him to try to make me chase something. I'm right. He throws it way outside; I watch it go by for ball one. He fools me on the next one—almost. It starts out looking like another fastball, but he's pulled the string. The ball floats to the plate. I start to go, but I don't. I wait, and swing, and drive it into the gap in left-center. By the time the center fielder chases it down, I'm standing on second, Woody's scored, and Nate's on third. We're ahead, 5-3. Mr. Conger sits, stony, and all I see under the cap is his jaw, set tight, a shadowy slit of a mouth, and darkness.

The Expos' manager walks out to talk with Gannon, who looks less confident as he listens, as he kicks dirt and waits.

Our guys start the Gra-dy chant in the dugout as Grady steps into the box and takes the first pitch for a ball.

"Not a batter, Gannon," Mr. Conger grunts. He's wrong, but he's right. Grady hammers the next pitch, but right at the shortstop.

Three outs.

Top of the fifth. My turn again. And Gannon's the first batter. My dad grins at me.

Our fans get loud. When the noise begins to die, I hear a voice: "No pitcher, Gannon," it says as Gannon steps into the box. "Noodle arm. No zip. No problem."

I look at Mr. Conger. His wife has her body angled away from him. I wish I could make him go away that easily.

Gannon settles in at the plate. I stare in, imagining Mr. Conger's face peering out from the pocket of Emmett's mitt.

I throw, but I'm not concentrating on my pitch, I'm concentrating on that face, and I let Gannon see the ball coming, big and fat and over the plate. He swings hard—that picture book swing of his—and the ball rockets away. I don't need to turn around to know its destination, but I do anyway. I watch Chas take a few steps back before he turns helplessly and follows the ball's flight, staring up and out, the way you'd look at a plane leaving a vapor trail in the sky. The ball clears the left-field fence and flies into the branches of a fir, twenty feet off the ground.

I watch as Gannon circles the bases, as he gets the congratulations of his teammates. We're only one run up, and it's my fault. I see Mr. Conger, standing, cheering for his kid. I spit into the dirt. I'm not going to let him wreck my game.

Emmett comes out. "You were kind of aiming that last one, Nelson," he says.

"I know," I say, and he heads back.

I stare in at him, imagining the mushy redness of the stump instead of Mr. Conger's face. I blow three screaming strikes past one batter, then another. The next guy grounds out to second.

"You'll get him next time," Sid says to me when we get to the dugout.

"Gannon, he could hit Randy Johnson's pitching," Chas says.

Bottom of the fifth. "Let's see if we can pad that lead a little," Mike says to us. But Chas goes down swinging, Webb pops to the catcher, and Sid bounces out.

Top of the sixth. The Expos' last at-bat. If we can keep them scoreless, it's simple: We win, *we're the champs.*

I'm feeling strong, maybe too strong. Suddenly every pitch is high. I walk the first two guys. A warm breeze kicks up, swirling dust from the third-base side out toward right field. My throat feels dry and half-clogged.

Raymond's up. I throw my heater for a called strike, then another. The runners steal second and third. I throw again, low and outside this time, but Raymond swings and misses. One out. The runners hold.

The next batter hits a high fly to fairly deep right. Woody settles under it, but I figure the Expos have the tying run; the guy on third will tag up and score once Woody makes the catch.

I wait, wishing the ball into his mitt, wishing he'll make the perfect throw, and can't believe what I see: *He doesn't make the catch.* Woody misjudges the ball; it bounces off his glove and drops behind him. By the time he gets it back to the infield, both runners have scored; the batter stands on third. It's Woody's error, but my fault the guys were on base. We're down, 6-5. I see our championship hopes fading. There's a guy on third and only one out, and the next two batters are a nightmare: Trey and Gannon.

I call time and motion for Emmett to come out. "Remember this guy from last time?" I ask.

"He chased a ball outside and low and pounded it into the dirt."

"I want to throw some inside strikes and get him to back off the plate, then go outside. But you need to know what's coming. We can't let the runner score from third."

"I'll expect inside stuff first," Emmett says. "Once you get two strikes on him, I'll move outside."

Emmett sets up a little inside. The mitt's in a perfect place; I just need to hit it. I throw the heater over the inside corner of the plate, moving Trey back.

"Strike!" the ump says.

I throw again: inside corner, a little high. Ball one, but Trey keeps his distance from the plate. Emmett stays inside, and I wind and pitch again. The ball moves a little inside, but the big guy goes for it and fouls it straight back. *Two strikes.*

Emmett shifts, moving to the outside edge of the plate. His mitt hovers knee-high, out of the strike zone. I hear the crowd, the players, but I shut them out. I picture the river, the second pile of rocks—my skipping stones. I remember my throwing motion—sidearm, releasing the stone low, skimming it over the surface of the river until it touched down.

I stare in toward Emmett, but see the riverbank, the brown water in between. I picture Emmett's mitt as the touchdown spot. I wind and throw, releasing the ball sidearm, watching it fly low, right to left, toward the plate at first but angling outside, heading for Emmett's mitt. Trey hesitates, then goes for it. He misses, nearly screwing himself into the ground. Strike three.

Emmett gives me the thumbs-up sign.

Gannon's up. Emmett sets up in the middle of the plate, and I throw. Ball one. I remind myself not to aim the ball. I picture that old stump one more time and throw my stump-blaster, rocketing it straight down the middle. For an instant I think it's past him, but his bat is lightning-quick. He drives the ball toward the right side of the infield, and I know it's trouble. I turn just in time to see Webb launch himself to his right, toward second base. Stretched completely out, both feet off the ground, he snares the ball backhand in the web of his glove. The ball sits there like a scoop of vanilla ice cream as he lands belly-first in the dirt, as dust rises around him. Smiling, he holds the ball high for the ump to see as our fans go wild.

"Out!" the ump says. Three outs. We're still only down by one.

Bottom of the sixth. Our last chance. The guys are grim-faced as we watch Gannon warm up, but then Mike does an impersonation of Mr. Conger.

"No pitcher," she says in a low-voiced growl, just loud enough for us to hear. "Noodle arm. No zip. No problem."

She grins at Hugh. "Start us off."

He does. He works the count to 3 and 2 before

letting a pitch go by that looks close. The ump calls it a ball. Hugh trots to first, and Webb and Sid go out to coach the bases.

"Stinking call, ump," Mr. Conger says. "You're killing us. Go back to tee-ball, where you belong."

The ump gives him a look; everyone gives him a look. He shuts up.

Emmett's up next. Mike stops him at the dugout entrance, her arm draped over his shoulders.

"What do you think about bunting, Emmett?" she says.

"I can bunt."

"If you get a pitch you like, consider laying one down. Okay?"

Emmett walks to the batter's box. He steps in, taking some big warmup swings.

"One-two-three, son," Mr. Conger says above the noise. "Easy pickings."

Emmett digs in, cocking the bat menacingly, but when the pitch comes, fast and down the middle, he suddenly squares and lays down a perfect bunt. Gannon gets to the ball, but he doesn't bother with a throw. We've got two runners on with no outs.

Woody goes to the plate. He swings and misses

twice. The third pitch bounces away from the catcher. Hugh steals third, Emmett second.

Two runners in scoring position now. If Woody can just manage a fly ball, we tie the game. A single could win it for us.

He takes a good cut but misses. Strike three. Now the Expos get loud.

"You moved 'em along," Nate says to Woody.

"You've got the bat, Nate baby," Mike tells Nate as he heads for the plate. "Just meet the ball and we'll be in business."

Nate settles in, taking cuts at an imaginary ball. I want him to smack the real one, to end the game. I'm up next; I don't want it to be up to me.

Nate hits the second pitch on the nose. Trey, who's playing first base, doesn't even have to move. The ball slams into his mitt for the out. He fakes a throw to second, but Emmett dives back; Hugh gets back to third. Two outs.

"If Gannon doesn't give you a good pitch, just settle for a walk," Mike tells me. "Grady's due to thump one."

Grady, on deck, smiles. "Just win it now, Nelson," he says. "Hit one for Andy Kirk."

I walk to the plate, breathing deep. My heart is booming.

"Gannon!" The voice is loud, unmistakable. Mr. Conger's. The other sounds die, like flames doused by some foul liquid. On the mound, Gannon turns and faces me, then kicks and scrapes at the dirt.

"Gannon!" the voice is louder. But Gannon ignores it. He finishes his dirt work and kicks his cleats against the rubber, then stares in at the catcher.

"Gannon!" Louder yet, like thunder, and Gannon looks; everybody looks. The game stands still as Mr. Conger bellows a command: "Down the heart, Gannon! Down the heart!"

I get a creepy cold feeling along my spine. I step out of the batter's box and look at Mike, who doesn't know about the secret code—the signal that means throw at the batter: me. But the guys gather around her. I know what they're saying, but what can she do? I look at the ump, but he's not the same ump who was there the day Mr. Conger got canned. This ump thinks down the heart means down the heart of the plate.

I move back into the box, giving the plate some room, getting a handle on Mr. Conger's dirty little scheme. All we need is two runs to win. Even just a single from me should score Emmett and Hugh from second and third, and we'll have what we need. But if Gannon hits me, he takes my bat away. He puts me on first base, where I can't hurt the Expos. Mr. Conger has decided to take his chances on Grady, who hasn't had a hit the whole game.

Mr. Conger's afraid of my bat, I decide. *He's afraid of my bat.* The idea warms me, it takes away some of the chill that's spread to my arms and legs. But now I can't think about swinging. I can only concentrate on bailing out if—when—the ball comes at my head.

Gannon winds, and I'm backing up before the ball even leaves his hand. It's a scorcher, but not inside, not at me. It blazes down the middle for a strike. Dust rises from the catcher's mitt as I stare at Gannon. I decide to set up closer to the plate.

"Down the heart!" Mr. Conger says. "Down the heart!" The voice is demanding, disappointed.

Gannon throws his heater again, but it's not a bean ball, it's not inside. It flies in low and outside for ball one. He gets the ball from the catcher and looks in again.

"Down the heart, Gannon!" The voice is raspy, louder, closer. I step out of the box and look behind me.

He's right there, at the backstop, his face flushed and angry under his Expos cap. "You hear me? Down the heart!"

The ump calls time. "The boy's doing his best, mister. You're interfering with the game. You need to get back to your seat." Mr. Conger doesn't move. "Or you can leave." They exchange a long, silent stare. Finally Mr. Conger returns to the bleachers.

I look out at Gannon, whose back is turned. He's facing the outfield, wiping at his face. I imagine going to the mound and asking him if he'd like to go with me and the rest of the guys to an empty field somewhere and just choose up sides and play for fun. But I know it's too late for that. I look at my dad, who's up on his feet, clapping. I hear him say Gannon's name, and then the rest of our fans are up, too. I hear my name, and Gannon's, and mine again.

"Play ball," the ump says, and Gannon sets himself on the mound. His face looks red and splotchy. I get back in the batter's box, not sure what to expect.

Gannon winds and throws. I fight the temptation to back out as the ball flies toward the plate. I don't. But it looks just a little inside, and I let it go.

"Strike!" the ump says. I turn to look at Mr. Conger,

silent, on his feet, fists clenched at his sides. Mrs. Conger glares up at him, her face a furious mask.

Gannon takes a deep breath, shakes out his shoulders, and faces the plate. But he looks past me, into the stands. He draws himself up to his full height, tips the bill of his cap back a little farther, and meets his father's gaze.

He shakes his head. No.

Now I know. Gannon isn't going to be throwing at me.

He and I are going to play the game.

I wait, certain he's going to bring his heater.

He winds, kicks, and delivers.

I see the ball, big and bright. No time to think, but I know it's coming fast and true, and I coil and swing hard to meet it.

I don't feel it on my bat but at the same time I do— that wonderfully rare bat-meets-ball connection when the bat seems to be made of some magic, honey-combed space metal, the ball of jumping beans and rubber.

For an instant I watch the ball as it leaps from the bat and climbs high over the shortstop's head. Then I'm off, churning for first, racing past Trey, who's looking toward left field, and Webb, waving me on. I make the turn, dimly aware of fan noise, and see Emmett approaching third. Where's the ball?

Nowhere. The center fielder jogs to a stop at the fence, joined by the left fielder. They're looking somewhere through it, over it, their shoulders slumped, and suddenly I know where the ball is: *home-run heaven.*

I plant my foot on second, but my feet barely kiss the ground as I sprint for third. Sid is there, clapping, smiling. "Slow down!" he shouts above the noise.

The guys are all out of the dugout, cheering me on as I round third. "Enjoy it!" Emmett yells from halfway down the third base line. I get to home plate, jump on it with two feet, and get mobbed. We win. *We're the champs.*

We regroup, and shake hands with the Expos, who mostly are trying to keep from crying but aren't having much success. They say some nice things. Gannon comes to me after everyone else. His eyes are red, his face smudged.

"Great game, Nelson," he tells me. "Killer home run."

"I think yours is still going," I say.

He shakes his head. "You hit my best pitch."

"Thanks for not throwing at me."

He shrugs. "I listened to my heart."

I remember the message. *Don't listen to the thunder. Listen to your heart.* I nod, wondering if I could have ignored that thunder.

"Your cousin—Mike—is she going to manage next year?" Gannon says.

"I hope," I say. She's standing at home plate, surrounded by all the guys, a giant grin on her face, wet streaks down both cheeks.

"I was thinking if we keep working, we should make Pony League next season. If Mike would manage, and we get you and me and some of the other guys on the same team, we'd be awesome."

"Unbeatable," I say.

"Talk to her," he says.

"I will."

I grab my gear and meet my mom and dad, who give me crusher hugs. We say good-bye to the rest of the guys and parents and head for the parking lot.

Just ahead of us, Mr. Conger trudges along. Mrs. Conger walks twenty feet in front of him, her arm around Gannon's shoulders. They lean to each other in conversation.

Mrs. Conger and Gannon stride past their car and continue on toward the park exit. Mr. Conger stops and stares after them. "The car," he says to their backs. "You went right by it."

Without stopping, Mrs. Conger turns and looks at him. "We'll walk home."

— 19 —
The Tree

June 14. The anniversary of Andy Kirk's accident. The last day of school. A half-day, mostly spent visiting.

Near the end of the morning, Mrs. King hands back a stack of assignments to each of us. My letter to Pecos Bill, written for our tall-tale project, is sitting on top of my stack of papers. "Original thought," Mrs. King has written on the top of it. "Excellent."

I look over at Emmett's papers as she sets them on our table in front of him. His letter to Paul Bunyan sits on top of his stack. "The depth of your thinking is impressive," she's written. "Outstanding." I decide *outstanding* is a notch above *excellent*, but I don't feel bad.

Mrs. King has corrected a misspelling on Emmett's paper. *There*, as in "The trees are *there* to prevent flooding, give us clean air, and provide a home for animals." Emmett has it spelled *their*.

I feel as if I've seen something I shouldn't have. I look at his face. His attention is on Mrs. King, who's talking. *There. Their.* How many people confuse them? A lot, probably. How many people on our team? One, at least.

"*Outstanding*," I say to Emmett, nodding at his letter. "Not bad."

"Thanks," he says. He glances at mine. "*Excellent* isn't too shabby."

"Just one misspelled word?" I say.

"I have trouble with that one."

"So did the ghost." He looks at me. "Twice," I say.

I wait for him to say something. Finally he smiles. "I like the idea of Andy Kirk's ghost," he says. "Maybe next season we'll be together on a different team with some different guys and we'll need some other messages."

I'm not sure what he's telling me. "Did you write 'em, Emmett?"

He smiles again. He shakes his head, just enough for me to notice. I don't know if he's telling me no, or if he's just done talking about it.

All around us kids are standing up, stuffing their belongings into their backpacks, chattering. They line up by the door as Mrs. King weaves her way through tables, giving directions, saying good-bye.

Finally the bell rings. I get on my bike and ride slowly toward the park.

No one's there when I arrive. Quiet sounds take over: birds, bugs, a frog, the air whispering past my ears as I point my bike toward the baseball diamond. No new messages.

I walk to the big cedar. Its lowest branch—the big, muscular limb with the elbow—is close to twenty feet over my head. From my backpack, I pull out a length of thick yellow rope with a weight tied to one end.

I underhand the weighted end over the branch. It heads down the other side. I let it drop, then slip the loose end of the rope through the hole in the weight and pull until the loop is tight around the branch, the weight hoisted snug against it.

I grasp the rope, then jump and grab on and pull up my feet. I climb until the limb is within reach. I take a big safety pin from my pocket and poke it through the two sections of rope where they meet at the weight, to keep everything from falling to the ground once I let go.

I grab the branch and swing my leg up and over. I smell the bark of the limb, pressed against my cheek. For the first time I look down—a long way down—and hug the branch tighter. *Beware of high limbs.* I feel blood pulsing through the vessels beneath my jaw. Finally I straddle the limb and sit up. The branch is solid, unmoving, as I scoot closer to the trunk.

I look out and see what I came to see: a perfect view of the diamond, the outfield. This was Andy Kirk's branch; I feel it.

A few seconds later I'm certain of it. A foot above the branch, carved into the ragged bark and brick-red wood of the trunk, are two-inch-high initials. They're weather-worn and partly barked-over, but unmistakable:

AK

I try to recall the shape of the initials on the messages. They're similar enough to make me feel as if my world has just suffered a deep-fault earthquake. A crack has opened somewhere; icy air seeps in.

I swing my left leg back so both feet are dangling over the same side and I'm facing the field. Perfect. I lean my left shoulder against the trunk for balance and wedge my hand into the crook of the limb.

I feel something loose against my fingers.

Coins. At the base of the branch, amidst the debris in a small hollow, are *coins.* I place them carefully on my thigh: two nickels, dated 1935 and 1940; two pennies, from 1939 and 1944. They're dark and discolored but otherwise perfect. *Andy Kirk's coins.*

But there are four coins, not five; two nickels, not three. I picture Andy reaching for another nickel as Sam crossed the plate with the go-ahead run. Was it at that moment that Andy lost his balance and fell? Is that nickel among the seven that were found, or is it still down there on the ground somewhere, the missing one? *Breathe,* I tell myself as I pick up the coins and shove them into my pocket.

A breeze stirs the branches of the big tree as my limb creaks beneath me. I plant both hands on its bark and wait for the breeze to die. But it doesn't die; it picks up, and suddenly it's a wind, gusting into me. For an instant I'm pushed back, off balance, and my stomach rises to my throat, but I lean tighter against the trunk and hold on.

The wind blows harder. All around me the trees wave their branches, showing off their shades of green and brown, their music of sighs and groans. The elbow of my limb bobs up and down in a kind of strange dance.

I twist to my right and straddle the branch again, facing out. The wind pushes steadily against me, but I lean forward and inch toward my rope. The sun disappears and the shade deepens around me. The rough bark pulls and scratches at the skin of my legs.

Grasping the rope, I let myself slip off the branch and hang. The rope swings back and forth like a pendulum. I pull the safety pin and let it drop before starting slowly down.

By the time I get to the ground the wind has grown fierce. I stuff the rope into my backpack. All around me, trees are swaying and complaining. I head for my bike, blown over and lying in the dirt. Dust swirls around me. Dark clouds balloon and billow and sink lower. The light behind the backstop flickers on. A big drop of rain splats against my neck.

I get on my bike and ride, pumping hard into the wind and rain. Halfway across the outfield I stop and look back at the trees. They're leaning side-to-side, forward and back; their boughs ripple like dark green water. But the big cedars stand fast. I shove off and pedal, legs straining, lungs aching, eyes blurring.

I stop and look up. I'm on the sidewalk in front of Wilson's Drug. My heart's throbbing, I'm sweating, steam rises from my wet shirt. People walk by, enjoying the sunshine, staring at me quizzically. Across the street at the post office, the flag hangs straight down, limp in the still air. I gaze back toward the park. The trees sway gently, then stop. It's just like Mike's story.

I reach into my pocket for the coins. They're there; I didn't imagine them.

But something is wrong; something turns my knees to soup. Everything around me fades to silence and shadow as I spread the coins across my trembling palm.

Two tarnished pennies. Two tarnished nickels. And a third nickel, gleaming in the sun. It looks out of place. I finger it, rotating it like a miniature wheel. It's shiny, yes, but not new. I stare at the date: 1946.

My breathing stops while I try to think. Was the nickel in my pocket when I climbed the cedar? Was it? A solitary, sparkling nickel from 1946?

I know the answer. *In my heart I know the answer.*